ILLUSIONS OF LOVE

ILLUSIONS OF LOVE

Sheila Spencer-Smith

CHIVERS

| British Library Cataloguing in Publication Data available |

This Large Print edition published by BBC Audiobooks Ltd, Bath, 2009.
Published by arrangement with the Author.

U.K. Hardcover ISBN 978 1 408 45672 9
U.K. Softcover ISBN 978 1 408 45673 6

11427197

Printed and bound in Great Britain by
CPI Antony Rowe, Chippenham and Eastbourne

A LOVE REMEMBERED

Carina Curnow emerged from her evening class, buzzing with exciting new prospects, only to stop in sudden dismay. There he was, leaning on the blue Honda Civic and smiling at her when he should have been on the other side of the world. 'Rob?' she called in disbelief as she moved towards him. 'What are you doing here?'

She felt the interest from her fellow students who were hovering about her. Local history? Forget it. Who wanted to dwell on the past when the present, in the shape of this man, bronzed and fair-haired, was likely to be so much more interesting?

'Jump in,' he said, pulling open the passenger door with a flourish. 'I've been sent to drive you home. Mum's busy preparing a feast.'

'But when did you get home? Why didn't you warn us?'

He laughed. 'And spoil the surprise? Come on, Carrie, jump in.'

She got into the car and they headed down Park Street as soon as she'd clicked her seat belt in place. Even after his time in New Zealand, Rob hadn't forgotten his way round Bristol's city centre, and Carina was impressed by his driving skills as he expertly eased the car

1

into the flow of traffic as they approached Temple Meads. In no time at all they were zooming round the Keynsham by-pass.

'I feel as if I'm being kidnapped,' Carina said.

'I'm after a hefty ransom,' Rob replied.

'Are you expecting Sadie to pay up?'

'For you, yes.'

The laughter in his voice was contagious and she smiled. 'Don't I get any say in this?'

'None,' he grinned. 'By the way, I noticed a sign to a new place on the way in, open air. Fancy a stop-off? We've got some catching up to do, Carina. I've missed you, you know.'

'You mean *The Lock Keeper*, down by the river? But Sadie's expecting us.'

'She won't mind,' Rob said with confidence.

He was right, Carina thought. If Rob was happy, then so was Sadie, his mother. And she would expect Carina, her equally loved ward she'd brought up from childhood, to be happy to fall in with his wishes, too.

Rob had been eight years old, Carina's senior by three years, when his parents had first taken her into the Mason home. Her young widowed father had gone off when she was five and it was then that Sadie and Max, her godparents, had taken her permanently into their care. The news came years later that her father had drowned in rough seas off the Sussex coast.

Sadie and Max considered Carina their own

2

daughter. When Max lay dying in hospital, he had taken Carina's hand and squeezed it, his way of saying how much she meant to them. Dear, kind Max! After all these years, she still missed him.

'Okay then,' she said now. *'The Lock Keeper* it is, but not for long.'

She glanced at Rob and saw the same lift of his chin and the way his hair waved at the back of his head as it had years ago, when she was fifteen. Her love for him then had been sudden and wonderful, and she had thought, from his friendly attentions, that he felt the same way about her. She had seen everything in heightened colours. The sun shone. She felt beautiful, her eyes shining when she looked in the mirror. Even her curly hair, usually so unmanageable, tamed itself into shining dark waves. Life, and Rob, were wonderful.

But Rob had never returned her feelings. And Carina could see now what a nuisance she had been to a young man about to set off for university, his sights set on a future that didn't include an infatuated fifteen-year-old girl. His patience with her dogged adoration finally snapped. She couldn't blame him for that, but she certainly blamed him for the way he had dealt with it at the time.

'Rob, listen,' Carina said now. 'You must remember what happened. And nothing's changed as far as I'm concerned.'

He slowed down at the roundabout. 'Oh,

3

come on, Carrie, that's water under the bridge, surely?'

'My silly infatuation? It's not that.'

'What then?'

Even now it was hard to get the words out. 'What you said then, about my not really belonging, not being one of the family.'

*   *   *

Rob drew into the side of the road, stopped the car, and turned to look at Carina. 'You mean that my careless remark of years ago still rankles in that pretty head of yours?'

'Careless remark? Hardly.'

'Really, Carina, it was years ago. And it didn't mean anything.'

Her lips tightened. No-one who came from a settled background could possibly understand what it felt like to be abandoned by a parent who should have had her interests at heart. At the time she had tried to tell Rob why she was upset and he had laughed at her for being so silly.

But her hurt was heart-deep, because she knew it was true. She didn't really belong. Not to anyone.

And, of course, this had helped make her what she was today; Carina Curnow, twenty-three years old and determined to make her own way in life.

'Don't be stupid, Carina,' Rob was saying.

'It was only words. Totally unimportant.'

'Is that how you see it . . . still?' Rob's lack of understanding hurt even more now. Suddenly she wanted to be anywhere but in this car with him.

They set off again. Rob took the next turning down a narrow lane, high-hedged and winding. He slowed down to go under the railway bridge and they came to the river and an expanse of grass. Nearby was a paved area attractively set out with picnic tables and chairs.

'Looks good,' Rob said, as they got out of the car. 'Shall we just sit out here, as we haven't got long? I'll take you to a fancy meal inside the restaurant another time, Carina.'

'If I'm still around,' she told him, as she moved towards the nearest table. Now where had that come from? Not really hard to tell, of course, after this evening's session at her class.

Carina gazed across the grass at the murky Avon. Day in, day out, forever flowing towards the sea, she thought, never changing. So it had been when they were both children and so it was now. She smiled, liking the thought of permanency.

Rob returned to their table with two huge mugs of cappuccino. 'There,' he said, seating himself opposite her. He scooped up a teaspoon of froth and gazed at it before putting it back where it came from.

'You always used to do that,' she said.

5

'And you used to wait until it was almost cold and then be surprised when you took a sip.'

'A long time ago,' she said.

'You could say that.'

She raised her spoon, and as she did so, a splash of liquid caught the front of her white T-shirt. With an exclamation of dismay, she dabbed at the brown stain with a tissue, making it worse.

Rob raised an amused eyebrow. 'Anyone would think you were still ten years old.'

'So what?' she said in response. 'I can throw cappuccino about if I want to.'

'Always the independent girl.'

She smiled. 'So what brings you back, Rob? Is it for good?'

'Aren't you pleased to see me? I expected a rapturous welcome.'

'Life has moved on .'

'And you're planning to move on, too?' He paused. 'Mum told me about the chap, Toby,' he went on gently. 'Don't look like that, Carrie. She said you're between relationships. No details.'

She felt warm colour flood her cheeks. 'He left Bristol, that's all. It finished. Sadie never liked him. It hadn't got very far, anyway. Nothing to worry about.'

'If you say so .'

She nodded and looked down at the teaspoon in her hand. It was true, what she

6

had said. Toby was no longer important, though for a while she had thought he might be.

'I had a fair whack of leave owing at the end of my New Zealand contract,' Rob told her. 'I can renew, of course, may well do so in due course. But a trip home was on the cards, so here I am.'

'All right for some,' Carina said. How she envied his easy assurance, his confidence. She began to stir her cappuccino as if she had a grudge against it.

'Hey, steady on,' he said, his eyes alight with amusement. 'What's it ever done to you?'

She put the spoon down. 'I was thinking,' she said.

'Deep thoughts?'

'Perhaps.' She raised her cup to her lips. The drink was comforting.

'I was sorry you were made redundant, Carina.'

'Not exactly redundant. I'm working as a temporary school secretary in various schools around here and I can do that on a permanent basis if I want to. But I don't think I do. Sadie thinks I should go for it as the salary's good, but money isn't everything?'

'You say that as if you really believe it.'

'Don't you think that there are things more important than money?'

'Maybe. Some things. Unless you don't have money, of course. So, what will you do now?'

7

'Nothing's finalised,' Carina said. How could it be, since she'd only just made up her mind after the information she'd been given this evening? A flicker of excitement ran through her. Now that Rob was here for a week or two, Sadie wouldn't be alone. The perfect opportunity.

And yet . . .

'You've changed, Carina,' Rob said. 'You know how to take life as it comes and act on it.'

'Maybe.' She wasn't sure he was right. It took a lot to motivate her. Living at home with Sadie was all she had wanted for a long time. She had convinced herself that this was because she owed Sadie a lot and it sounded good to say she was looking after her. But maybe it was just an excuse not to move out of a safe environment.

'You've been away three years,' she reminded Rob. 'Of course I've changed.'

Rob had changed, too. She shivered a little in the cooling air. The hills on the other side of the river were darkening now.

'We're still friends though, aren't we?' he said.

'Haven't we always been?'

'My two favourite people!' Sadie greeted them as they pushed open the door of the tall, white

8

house in Welton Street. She was wearing her best strappy shoes, her new white jeans and a colourful top Carina hadn't seen before. 'You look wonderful,' she said. The next moment, she was nearly swung off her feet in a hug. Laughing, she extricated herself. Sadie was a good six inches shorter, a good deal plumper, too. 'Watch it, Sadie, you'll do yourself an injury,' she cried, laughing.

'Not today, love,' Sadie said. 'Nothing can hurt me today. Not now my Rob's home.'

It was Rob's turn now and he hugged his mother tightly.

Carina gazed round her at the vases of pink roses on the hall table and the window sill.

Sadie, noticing, smiled. 'I just had to rush out and get them,' she said. 'I knew Rob wouldn't care one way or the other, and I know that New Zealand's full of much more exotic blooms, but I just had to do it to show how delighted I am to have him home.'

From Sadie's glowing appearance, no-one could doubt her feelings for her son, and Carina felt an overwhelming love for her.

'I'd have brought you pink roses if I'd known you wanted them, you daft woman,' Rob said.

'And for Carina too, I hope,' said Sadie.

Rob smiled. 'Masses of them.'

'So what do you think of our Carina, Rob? Hasn't she grown into a beautiful girl?'

Warm colour flooded Carina's cheeks at the

admiration in Sadie's voice. She didn't wait to hear Rob's reply, but rushed upstairs to change out of her coffee-stained top, grabbing the first shirt that came to hand.

There was the murmur of voices from the sitting room as she went downstairs and she found Rob and Sadie seated on the wide sofa beneath the window. Since it took up nearly all the space in the small room, there was no other furniture apart from a bookcase and a couple of small tables. Sadie patted the space at her side.

'Come and hear what Rob's telling us about New Zealand,' she said. 'The adventure school he's helped set up sounds wonderful.'

This was safe ground at least and Carina was able to listen and comment. At the same time, she wondered how Sadie would react when she heard of her own future plans.

*   *   *

Sadie rose to clear the plates from the table after they had enjoyed the chicken dish she had so lovingly prepared. 'That was great, Mum,' Rob said, leaning back in his chair with both hands behind his head. 'Worth coming home for.'

'But not the only thing worth coming for, surely,' said Sadie, glancing at Carina.

'But I'm too late, Mum. She's running away.'

Sadie paused with the pile of plates in her hand. 'Carina, what's Rob talking about? You'd never leave home just because he's back with us?'

Carina took the plates from her, carried them into the kitchen and put them down on the new granite worktop Sadie was so proud of.

'You're serious about leaving home?' Sadie said, stricken. 'But you can't even think of such a thing. Oh dear, I hoped . . . '

She broke off, obviously upset.

'Please, Sadie, don't let's talk about it now. I'll fill you in later on what I discovered tonight at my class, I promise. I haven't thought it through properly yet, but you'll be the first to know what I decide. I just need to . . . ' It was Carina's turn now to feel tearful. She hated upsetting Sadie and wished Rob had kept quiet, so she could choose a better time to discuss her plans.

Sadie took a deep breath. 'I've made an apple pie, Rob's favourite,' she said, her voice slightly shaky.

Carina gave her a hug. 'Sadie, I need to know you're happy about it or I'll forget the whole thing.'

'I'm a selfish old woman,' Sadie said.

Carina smiled. 'Selfish? No way. And old? Rubbish. Look at you in that lovely get-up. You look like a young thing.'

Sadie gave a tearful giggle.

11

'And if I hadn't been offered a house to live in, with the sea on the doorstep and clifftops to explore, I wouldn't be thinking of moving an inch.'

AN INTRIGUING DISCOVERY

Carina closed the front door behind her the next morning and paused for a moment to enjoy the fresh air. The sound of traffic was muted and a soft breeze stirred her hair as she walked along the narrow street into the broader one that led to the park.

Sadie had already left for her job in the Post Office half an hour before. She had gone off cheerfully enough, trim in her RSPB sweatshirt and navy skirt, even though it was Saturday morning and she would much rather have been at home now her son was here. Carina was aware that she expected the two of them, left behind, to spend the day in each other's company. Not a good idea. In any case, Rob would most likely want a lie-in to recover from his journey.

Whether it had been jet lag or not, something had made him light-headed enough yesterday evening to assume he and Carina were going to start up some sort of relationship.

And Sadie hadn't helped, either. The

pressure had been on all evening and Carina hadn't liked it one little bit. Feeling stifled, she had hugged to herself the knowledge of the house on the cliff-top, imagining the roar of the waves and the feel of the salty air on her face.

It wasn't until the kitchen clock had struck eleven that Sadie had said, 'I can't believe you really want to desert us, me and Rob. Let's talk about it tomorrow afternoon when I get back from work, shall we?'

*   *   *

Carina glanced at her watch. Too early to visit her friend, Annabel, for coffee, as they had planned, but it felt good to be out of the house this warm spring morning. The birds were filling the air with exultant song and sunlight and shadows made patterns on the path. The willow branches draping the edge of the lake were already green.

It was great that Rob was home again, of course, but Sadie's dream of the two of them getting together romantically was not on. For one thing, she and Rob were just friends, and had been for years. For another, being pressurised into something, even if it had been the desire of her heart once, felt wrong. There were some things that you had to come to yourself and love was one of them.

She came to a seat, damp with dew, pulled

13

off her waterproof jacket and sat on it. She hated hurting Sadie by seeming to be anxious to be gone, but in the circumstances, life at number 77 was likely to be a strain for the next week or so. And now Carina had the perfect reason for leaving, one that even Sadie might approve of.

Annabel's flat was on the top floor of a block that had been built on the waterfront several years ago. Carina, with a pleasant feeling of anticipation, entered the waiting lift and pressed the button for the third floor. She had so much to tell Annabel. Friends since primary school days, they had kept in touch through Annabel's training as a nursery nurse and her own at secretarial college, from where she had emerged to work as one of the school secretaries at the local comprehensive. Now, her job at the school was being merged with another, and she had been invited to re-apply along with three others who had been in their positions for much longer than Carina had. Annabel, her loyal friend, was highly indignant on her behalf and urged immediate action, without being able to suggest what that should be. Carina smiled as she imagined telling her friend of the job offer that had been made to her yesterday evening and which she was seriously considering.

14

'Come on in,' said Annabel, throwing open her door as Carina emerged from the lift. Her sitting-room looked as welcoming as ever with its cheerful yellow walls and bright furnishings.

Carina went in and raised an eyebrow in pretend criticism of her friend's new outfit. 'Wow!'

'Like it?' said Annabel, twirling round so that the short skirt flared out in a swirling mass of colour.

'It's colourful,' said Carina. 'Bright purple with a red top'

'Not red. Fuchsia, please, the in-colour for the in-people.'

Carina smiled. 'Whatever you say.' Her own jeans and white T-shirt looked dull in contrast, but that was the way she liked it. 'You're the one needing to make an impression at that school of yours,' said Annabel.

'Not any more,' Carina replied. She slung her jacket on a handy chair and sat down on the window seat, her favourite place. She took a quick look at the view over the river to the spire of St Mary Redcliffe that dominated the skyline, and then turned back to her friend. 'I've got something astounding to tell you, Annabel. But first, what d'you think? Rob's home.'

'The wonderful Rob?' Annabel plonked herself down on the sofa. 'How is he? Still the glamour boy? But that's great! How long is he home for?'

'A few weeks. Sadie's delighted.'

'And you?'

Carina frowned. 'Glad to see him, of course.'

'But?'

'But he seems to have ideas about the two of us and Sadie is encouraging him.'

'What sort of ideas? I thought you couldn't stand each other?'

'That was years ago,' said Carina.

'Says you.'

'Don't you believe me?'

Annabel sighed. 'Wishful thinking. He's simply gorgeous. Just point him in this direction if you don't want him.'

Carina laughed. 'The point is, the atmosphere at home is thick with plans and I don't like it.'

'So what's the problem? Move out into a place of your own. Like me.' Annabel looked round at the large living space she had made so much her own.

'It's not as simple as that, Annabel. You know it isn't. Sadie would be deeply hurt, and after all she's done for me, I don't want that.'

'So what's the answer?'

'Something I found out yesterday at my local history class. The tutor, Martin, was showing us how to check the 1901 census to discover who lived then in the houses in certain streets. He let us all have a go to see if we could turn up anything about our families.

16

Not much good for me, though, because Sadie's family isn't mine. I told him that.'

'And?'

'He said my surname was unusual. Worth investigating. So he typed it in, and, Annabel, what do you think? It came up with my father's name, Vyvyan Curnow, and the place in Cornwall where he was born.'

'Hey, wait a minute. 1901? Your father? Even if he was a baby then, it would make him a hundred and seven if he was still alive today, at the very least. And you'd be in your seventies. Carina.'

Annabel gazed at her, laughing, her head held to one side. 'I must say, you don't look it.'

'Thanks.'

'So who is this Vyvyan Curnow, then?'

'I've no idea. He can't be my dad. Dad was born in 1950. But they've got the same name. Strange, don't you think? It could mean we're related somehow, though.'

'He could be your dad's father?'

A shimmer of excitement ran through Carina. 'My grandfather?'

'Could be, if he married late. It's possible. He would have been forty-nine in 1950, if you think about it. His wife could have been a lot younger.'

'And by the time I was around he'd have been . . . what . . . eighty-four? But dad never talked about him.'

'Could have passed away by then?'

17

'There's more to tell you, Annabel,' Carina said. 'Someone at the class heard us talking.'

'Never!'

'I won't tell you if you can't be serious?'

Annabel adopted a solemn expression but her eyes were dancing. 'Go on then, Carina. This person told you that he knows the Curnows, that you've got relations you didn't know existed, cousins . . .'

'Don't be silly. You know my parents were only children, so I haven't any aunts or uncles. Or cousins, come to that. No, it's not that.'

'What then?'

'There's a job going . . . looking after holiday apartments, seeing people in, that sort of thing. Seasonal, of course.'

'In the place your father was born?'

'Well, not exactly. But Newquay's not all that far from Poltizzy.'

'Poltizzy? What sort of name's that?'

'Normal, if you're in Cornwall.'

'And you soon will be, by the sound of it. Oh Carina, that's perfect. You'll be able to do some research on the 1901 Vyvyan Curnow and maybe find your real family.'

'Sadie and Max have always been my real family.'

'And Rob?'

Carina sighed. 'Yes, and Rob.'

Annabel leaned forward in her chair, her face so full of concern that Carina was touched. 'You must want to find out more if you've decided to go for this job.'

'I'd like to see the house where my father was born,' Carina admitted. 'The 1901 Vyvyan Curnow may be long forgotten, though.'

'You can check,' Annabel said. 'There'll be a record office somewhere in Cornwall.'

'I'll be working hard,' Carina pointed out. 'The season's just starting and there'll be masses to do by the sound of it. In any case, I haven't got the job yet. I've got this phone number to contact, the sister of my pal at the class. She married a Cornish chap and they set up this mini business letting out their holiday properties to holidaymakers. They need people working for them, cleaning and everything. And someone to be in overall charge.'

'You?'

'Maybe, if I'm suitable.

'Phone now,' said Annabel.

The traffic was light and they made good time on the journey down to Cornwall. Carina, still shell-shocked by the speed everything was happening, was in the passenger seat of Annabel's Fiesta. Their overnight bags were on the back seat, together with a couple of sleeping bags, just in case. Carina had left a note for Sadie and a message on her voice mail, planning to phone her again when she knew she would be home.

'This is the life,' Annabel said, opening the window and exulting in the wind on her face. 'I wish it was me being interviewed for the job, as well as you.'

'Belinda sounded okay on the phone,' Carina said. 'Belinda Penberthy. She was glad I could visit at once so she could meet me. And she wants me to see what's involved before I take the job on.'

'Sensible,' Annabel agreed.

'Thanks for driving me down,' said Carina.

'That's what friends are for.'

'I'm going to miss you, Annabel. If I get the job.'

'Me too,' said Annabel. 'And of course you'll get the job. And I'll be down all the time to see you, don't worry.'

'The busy time for me will be weekends.'

'I might as well turn round and head for home then, if there's going to be no chance of free holidays!'

'Don't you dare!'

They reached the turn-off they were told to take, and soon saw the sea ahead of them and sunlight glinting on white buildings. They had been three hours on the road, stopping only once for petrol and to get a coffee and sandwiches.

'I'm beginning to feel nervous,' Carina said. She delved in her bag and pulled out the notepad on which she had jotted down the directions. She was due to meet Belinda Penberthy at three o'clock and it was nearly that now. 'Parking's tricky, apparently. There's one place allocated to the apartment we're heading for, so she'll leave that clear for us,' Carina said.

They were nearing the town now and Carina leant forward to check the next signpost. 'Yes, that's it. Straight across here and right at the next roundabout. It's easy from there. Follow the signs for the surfing beach and turn right just before we get there.'

'Well, that makes sense,' said Annabel.

Carina laughed, more relaxed now they were nearly there.

Belinda Penberthy glanced askance at Annabel's colourful skirt and skimpy top. 'Carina Curnow?'

'That's me,' said Carina, stepping forward. The expression on the older woman's face changed quickly to one of welcome. 'Hello, Carina. Glad to meet you. I'm Belinda. Come in, both of you.'

Carina smiled, liking the pleasant face and comfortable build of the woman she had come to meet. She had envisaged a high-powered businesswoman instead of someone dressed in flapping corduroy trousers that looked none too clean.

21

'Ask her if she knows your family,' Annabel hissed, as she followed Carina into the apartment.

'Stop it,' said Carina. 'This is an interview.'

Carina frowned a warning to Annabel and turned to exclaim at the view. From one of the windows on the long wall of the spacious room she could see right up the coastline to a lighthouse on a distant headland. The patio doors gave access to a balcony with a view over an expanse of grass to the beach and a small headland jutting out into the azure sea.

'As you can see, the kitchen area is this end of the room,' said Belinda, indicating a well-planned area of units. 'Open plan. Our guests seem to like it.'

'I should think they do,' Annabel said. 'You're lucky, Carina.'

'She'll be working here cleaning the place, not in residence,' said Belinda, her voice sharp. She threw a glance of dislike at Annabel, who had the sense to keep well back as they viewed the rest of the apartment. In a business-like way, Belinda explained where the cleaning materials were kept and what would be expected of anyone who worked for her.

'There are four apartments, two in this block and two in the next,' she said. 'We have four cottages on the other side of the bay as well. You have your own transport?'

'Well, no,' Carina said. 'Not at the moment. Is that a problem?'

'You have a clean driving licence?'

Carina nodded. 'Oh yes. I can show you.'

'That won't be necessary.'

'Why not?' Annabel said.

'It's vitally important for our guests to display their parking permits in their cars at all times,' Belinda said, ignoring her. 'You must make that quite clear to them, Carina. Last year, one car got clamped and the owner was charged a great deal of money.'

'Bad for business,' Carina said.

'Exactly.'

*   *   *

'An army of desperate clampers prowling the streets,' Annabel muttered, as they left the apartment and walked behind Belinda down the stairs. 'A dangerous place to be, this.'

Belinda was going into more detail about the job, explaining that the lettings were over three days, Fridays, Saturdays and Sundays. 'The properties aren't all necessarily let at the same time,' she said, smiling at Carina as they reached Annabel's car. 'Though of course, we'd like them to be. I'll give you a copy of the chart and you can work out a system. Sometimes there will be someone to help you, but I'm looking for a person to be in overall charge. I'll need references, of course, and you'll need time to consider.'

'If you want me, I'll have to give notice at

work.' Carina said.

'Our first booking is for next Friday week. So . . . shall we leave it at that then, and we'll be in touch?'

'Of course' This seemed hopeful, Carina thought, but you could never be sure.

'You're not planning on driving back tonight?' Belinda glanced into the back of the car. 'Sleeping bags? You can kip down at my place, Spray Point, if you like. There's not much room, as we use the place mainly for storage, but you're welcome to find a space somewhere on the floor.'

'Thanks. We'd be glad to. We were planning to sleep in the car,' Carina said.

'Follow me, then. I'm parked round the corner.'

A LINK TO THE PAST

As they drove slowly up the uneven track, Carina glanced up at the white bungalow on the high ground above them. It looked as if it had been standing there for years, enduring everything the elements could throw at it. Spray Point wasn't exactly on a point, as Carina had imagined, but its location was almost as spectacular and the roar of the waves rolling in to the long stretch of beach on their right was deafening. Annabel turned sharply to the left and drove up to a steep tarmacked area to park the car behind Belinda's van.

Dragging bags and sleeping bags behind Belinda up the steep path nearly took their breath away and they stood panting at the top while Belinda thrust the key in the lock. She leant her shoulder against the door and pushed it open with difficulty. The smell of stale air met them as she ushered them inside.

'Leave the door open,' she said. 'We'll open some windows and get fresh air swirling about the place. Sorry about the mess.'

The entrance hall was home to three massive wardrobes as well as a large table piled high with duvets and bedding sets. More were stacked on chairs. Three divan beds, folded, leaned against one wall. Someone had hung a clothes airer with so many towels that it sagged alarmingly and seemed in danger of collapsing. Even Annabel was speechless as she stood hugging her belongings.

Belinda waved her hand apologetically. 'We're still fitting out the four cottages and it all takes time,' she said. 'This is the only place to store all this for the moment.'

'You've got only four cottages?' Annabel said in surprise. 'I'd have guessed at least six from this lot.'

'My husband was in the process of negotiating another purchase,' Belinda said tartly.

25

'Was?'

'He's in hospital'

'Oh. Sorry,' Annabel said.

Through an open door Carina saw more bedding piled on a sofa and armchairs. Beyond were the windows and she exclaimed in delight. 'Just look at the view!' She went into the room for a better look, with Annabel close behind.

'So we've got something right?'

Dismayed at the hurt in Belinda's voice, Carina turned to her hastily. 'This is a wonderful place and I can see the potential,' she said. 'I can see that it's useful for accumulating stuff here temporarily. I'd kill for such a view.'

Somewhat mollified, Belinda smiled at her. 'Lovely, isn't it? That's the lighthouse on Trevose Head you can see in the distance.'

'And what are all those black things in the sea?' asked Annabel.

Belinda was dismissive. 'Surfers. You'll get used to seeing them when the surf's right. Look, dump your stuff in here and I'll show you the kitchen.'

Although in a bit of a mess, there was no extra furniture stored in the room at the back, only bags of household items obviously destined for kitting out the other properties.

'We'll have a bedroom free for you by the time you come,' Belinda said. 'We live elsewhere, my husband and I, and let our staff take over *Spray Point* for the season if they need accommodation.'

'It sounds as if my friend's got the job then,' Annabel said.

For the first time Belinda smiled at her. 'It all depends if she wants it.'

'And if my references are up to scratch,' Carina said. It seemed that life here would be more of a challenge than she had thought. And such a contrast to her life in Sadie's comfortable home. My home, she reminded herself. Rob's too, for the moment.

'I'll leave you then,' said Belinda. 'Just make yourselves at home. Plenty of eating places in town if you're hungry. I take it you'll be off fairly early in the morning? The key's in the lock. Post it through the letter box when you go.'

'Of course,' Carina assured her.

'We won't waste time eating,' Annabel said when they had cleared a space on one of the bedroom floors and unrolled their sleeping bags. 'Poltizzy, here we come!'

'You are joking,' Carina said.

'Never been more serious.'

'But is there time to explore now? We don't know exactly where it is, or how far.'

'There's a map in the car. Come on, Carina, it's what we've come down here for, isn't it?

We can't pass off a chance like this. Belinda might not offer you the job, and what then? This will be a wasted journey if we don't fit in a visit to your ancestral home.'

'You're persuading me,' said Carina, smiling.

'So has it worked?'

'Why not? Poltizzy, here we come!'

*   *   *

As the car bounced down the stony track, Carina gazed at the huge waves rolling in to the shore, which was dotted with surfers. There were so many of them, and they looked like black seals having the time of their lives. She could see the fascination, the freedom, the extraordinary feeling of achievement in catching a wave at just the right moment and riding it upright, swaying this way and that to get the longest run. She thought of Rob and wondered if the surfing in New Zealand was as good as this. Better, probably. At the adventure base, they would surely have surfing in the programme as well as all the other activities he'd been so enthusiastic about last night, bungee jumping being one of them. She shuddered.

'What's up?' asked Annabel, slowing down at a roundabout. 'Don't you want to see Poltizzy?'

'Yes, of course I do. How far is it?'

'About ten miles. Not far once we get on to the main road.'

Soon they had left the town behind. 'Seems a long way,' Annabel commented. 'Look out for the turning to Madrenna somewhere on the right.'

Carina, concentrating on signposts that were few and far between, was hardly aware of the distance they had come. 'There it is!' she cried. 'And Poltizzy's on the sign, too. Two and a half miles.'

Annabel slowed down now they were in narrow, high-banked lanes that twisted and turned. Then they were there. Poltizzy.

The village turned out to be a few old cottages with a line of newer terraced ones at the end. A building, once the school, had been converted into a village hall and stood a little way back from the road. Next to it was a small shop, obviously closed, with a post box outside.

Annabel drove along slowly, and Carina felt awe steal over her as she gazed around her. Here her father had grown up, played with friends, walked to school . . . Dad had never spoken of it to her and she wondered why. Of course, she hadn't been very old when he had left home, but surely she would have remembered such an unusual name? 'Poltizzy,' she murmured. The name sounded magical to her even now.

'How on earth are we to know where Poltizzy House is?' Annabel said. 'We'll have to ask. Look, there's someone going into that cottage. She'll know.' She stopped the car and wound down the window.

The white-haired person, stooping a little, turned towards them. 'Can I help, m'dear?' she asked in a friendly voice.

'We're looking for Poltizzy House,' said Annabel. 'Do you know where it is and who lives there?'

'You're looking for old Mr Curnow then? He don't live there no more. Up on the hill near Madrenna, that's where he be now.'

'In the churchyard?' said Annabel, appalled.

A deep rumbling laugh shook the bent figure. 'Don't you let him hear you say that, my lover. Madrenna Nursing Home, that's where Taryn Curnow lives now. Ninety-eight years old last Friday. That's some age. Can't manage the old house no more, you see.'

'I knew a Vyvyan Curnow,' Carina said, leaning across her friend. 'I didn't know there were any others in the family.'

A loud barking broke out from a nearby house and the woman turned away. 'Good day to you, m'dears. That's all I can tell you about the old gentleman.'

Annabel watched her go. 'She didn't tell us how to find the house'

'Poor old man,' said Carina. 'Having to move out of his home because he's old and all alone.'

'But he's gone to a place nearby to be well

taken care of,' Annabel pointed out. 'What's wrong with that? At ninety-eight, he should count himself lucky.'

'Ninety-eight,' said Carina, considering. 'Born about 1910. That's amazing. He must have been the brother of Vyvyan Curnow, who was a baby at the time of the 1901 census.' She turned a radiant face to Annabel. 'I must go and see him.'

'Why not? They'll have visiting hours, I suppose.'

'It'll be back there,' said Carina. 'That big house on the bend in the lane. There's a board outside, and I'm sure it said Madrenna Nursing Home.'

The following week flew by so swiftly that Carina hardly had time to draw breath. On Monday, Belinda rang with a firm offer of the job and Carina accepted. They arranged to meet at *Spray Point* on the Saturday. She would enquire about coach travel from Bristol, or she might travel by train, if that was possible.

Working her notice out by day, gave Carina little time to decide what she needed to take with her for several weeks down in Cornwall. And there were friends to meet and say goodbye to before she left. Rob, too, wanted to be with her and Sadie planned a special meal for the three of them and Annabel on her last evening home. Annabel, however, had already made other plans and to her regret had to refuse. Sadie didn't sound too upset, though. She would now have Carina and Rob all to herself this last evening. 'Annabel will be able to visit you down there, I expect,' she said, as she laid the table in the dining room with her best damask cloth.

'And so can you, Sadie,' Carina said, giving her a hug. 'I shall count on it. Plenty of birds down there for you to watch through those fine binoculars Rob gave you. Your bird-watching group will be green with envy.'

Sadie glanced at the binoculars sitting in pride of place on the top of the piano. 'Aren't they great?' she said. She reached for the box of red table mats and extracted the number she needed. 'Tell me again about the place you're staying at, Carina. Is it really as good as it sounds?'

'*Spray Point?* Actually, it's better than I thought it would be, or will be when Belinda's got it sorted out.' Carina took the mats from Sadie and laid them in place on the table. 'Sadie, you're being so good about this and I do appreciate it. I was so afraid you'd feel hurt.'

'I know how much it means to you, love.'

Carina smiled. 'You can imagine, too, how I felt when I heard about the Mr Curnow in the nursing home. He must be the same family, mustn't he?'

'It sounds like it,' said Sadie, pausing before opening the cutlery drawer. 'I know your father was born at Poltizzy House. Your mother never actually saw the place because she and your dad met when they were both working here in Bristol. That's when Max and I first met them and became close friends.'

'But you never spoke of Poltizzy.'

'There was no reason to,' said Sadie sadly. 'I wish we had now. Then I could tell you more and be of some use.'

'But you are of use,' Carina said. 'You've been marvellous about everything. And look at the encouragement you've given me, though you must think I'm mad taking this job miles from home just to be able to follow up a tenuous link with the past.'

'Maybe not so tenuous now you've found out about Mr Curnow,' Sadie said. 'I'm pleased for you and I do understand, love. We all need to know where we came from.'

'It would be wonderful to find out,' Carina mused.

'And it's only a seasonal job after all,' Sadie pointed out. 'Your home will always be here.'

'Of course it will.'

Sadie looked sad for a moment. 'It's just bad timing, when Rob's come home for a holiday, but that can't be helped. Ah, here he is now.'

'Something smells good,' Rob said as he

33

came into the room.

Carina smiled at him as she helped lay the cutlery in place. 'We were just talking about the old man in the nursing home who might turn out to be a relation of mine.'

'Or might not,' said Rob. 'Cornwall's seething with old men, I shouldn't wonder. All those old salts down on quaysides mending fishing nets and swapping yarns with gullible tourists.'

'He's so rude, my son,' Sadie said fondly.

Rob pulled out a chair and sank down on it with his long legs stretched out in front of him. 'Bring on the food, slaves. I'm starving.'

Laughing, they did as he said. Sadie's beef stew was one of Rob's favourites and cooked tonight at his request. Apple meringue and trifle followed and then Carina made coffee that they drank sitting at the table, too full and lazy to move into the sitting room.

'It was such a disappointment when we found we couldn't visit the nursing home,' said Carina, as she poured the coffee. 'They're strict with visits when the patient isn't well. He's had flu, poor old man. Thank goodness he's on the mend. I'll be able to visit him when I get down there.'

'I hope you're not disappointed, love,' said Sadie as she added milk and passed the jug across the table to Rob.

'Do they have birds down there?' asked Rob, as he spooned sugar into his cup.

'Seabirds, I suppose. Albatross? Deep-throated Flapper Birds, Lesser Spotted Welly-Woolies?'

'Don't be ridiculous,' said Sadie.

'Ridiculous, is it? You should get your bird-watching crew interested, Mother. Maybe fix up one of your bird-watching weekends down there to check out the local bird population. Feathered ones, that is.'

'We saw a spoonbill on the Exe estuary the weekend before last.'

'Spoonbill? What sort of self-respecting bird would have a name like that? Humiliating, I should think, being named after a personal characteristic. You might just as well have called me Handsome Face or Perfect Physique.'

Carina giggled.

'Spoonbills are rare these days, I'll have you know' Sadie got up to pull down the blind in the side window against the setting sun. She yanked the cord hard and when she returned to her chair, Carina saw a suspicious glitter in her eyes. Couldn't Rob see he wasn't helping matters with his silly talk?

'Oh, Sadie, I meant to ask you something.' *What, what? Quick, think of something.* 'Sadie, my birth certificate. We've got it somewhere, haven't we?'

Sadie's face brightened. 'Of course. It's in the bottom drawer of the bureau in the other room. I should have thought of something as

35

vital as that. I do wish there was more I could find for you.'

'Such as what?' said Rob, leaning back in his chair. 'Carina's face is her fortune. What more does she want?'

Ignoring him, Sadie got up. 'I'll get it now while I think of it.'

Rob sat up as soon as she left the room, the expression on his face earnest. 'I could borrow Mum's car and run you down to this place after taking her into work. No problem. Make things much easier and I could suss it out for you, make sure you're doing the right thing. What d'you say?'

'No, really, Rob. This is the way I want it.'

'Struggling with all your gear on public transport?'

She nodded. 'Mad as it sounds, it's important to me. Annabel offered to drive me but I refused. This is my thing, Rob. Something I must do on my own.'

The last thing Carina needed was Rob putting the pressure on. He might even take a bad report of *Spray Point* back to Sadie and she would worry. No, she had to be on her own in this.

'I'll do that gladly.'

TROUBLE FOR CARINA

Carina stood at the window at Spray Point and gazed out at the headland on the other side of the bay. The sea was calm today, with tiny waves breaking unevenly on the thin strip of beach. Even so, some hopeful surfers were in the water, floating on their boards.

'They never give up,' Belinda said.

'They must be keen,' Carina replied. The sea was flat, for goodness' sake. Were they expecting a sudden storm to send the breakers roaring in so that they could all spring upright and ride the waves back to the shore?

'I'll leave you now,' said Belinda. 'Your phone's switched on?'

Carina smiled. 'I'll be here, ready and waiting for the call.'

Belinda nodded and looked at her watch. She was wearing a baggy grey T-shirt and a long skirt that sagged at the back. Maybe this was her best outfit, Carina thought. At least it was clean.

The interior of *Spray Point* looked less like a furniture depository now than it had a week ago. The bedroom at the back, which was allocated to Carina, held a single bed, wardrobe and chest of drawers. Someone had been working hard emptying the place and kitting out the four cottages ready for occupation. Carina wondered if more than one of them was to be occupied today.

She had arrived early this afternoon and had been met at the station by Belinda in the van.

'You'll have *Spray Point* to yourself for a day or two,' Belinda had said, heaving Carina's bags into the back and slamming the door. 'Not a problem, I trust?'

'Not a bit,' said Carina, climbing into the passenger seat.

'You'll need to get stuck in at the cottages tomorrow. All the furniture's in place. Two of them are ready for occupation, but the others need cleaning from top to bottom.'

Belinda nodded as she put the van into gear and they set off. 'The family coming into one of the apartments today is from Oldham. They've booked the one you saw when you came down. Arriving some time this afternoon, fairly late. Mother, father and two children. I've instructed them to phone your mobile when they get to Penwick. That'll give you ample time before they arrive to get over to let them in. Think you can do that?'

'Of course.'

Now, looking out at the sea, Carina felt nervous. Belinda obviously felt that throwing her in at the deep end was best, and had just left her to it. But suppose there were difficulties . . . suppose the people didn't like the apartment and blamed her . . . suppose they got lost . . . didn't turn up . . . anything? But this was stupid. There was no reason at all why things shouldn't go as smoothly as Belinda expected. This was merely Carina's nerves talking.

She checked that her mobile was switched on and then replaced it in the pocket of her jeans.

Carina took the steps down to the beach two at a time and nearly collided with a wet-suited surfer climbing up. His face was glowing with health and vitality and he smelt of the sea.

'No harm done,' he said, as she blurted out an apology before rushing off.

Although Belinda had assured her she had plenty of time to greet the new arrivals after receiving their phone call, Carina raced across the beach and arrived, breathless, in the car park for the apartments. She stood leaning against the wall to recover her breath and then had to wait a further nervous ten minutes before the holidaymakers drove up. Typical. Annabel would have belted up at the last minute, smilingly delighted to see the family, instead of being all tense and anxious because of having to hang around. But this was Carina's first time and she wanted to make a good impression.

She needn't have worried. The family was

delighted to be met and delighted with the apartment. Carina felt as pleased as if she had organised the place herself, instead of merely being the person who let them in. She smiled at the excitement of the two little girls as they rushed from room to room.

Then she left them to it.

*   *   *

The late afternoon sun felt pleasantly warm as Carina walked down the road to the beach. There was definitely a buzz at being on the receiving end of such delight. One of the perks of the job, she supposed.

She had time now to look about her at the surfing at this end of the beach. There were surfers everywhere, some changing in the car park, others returning hired boards, others still in the sea. She walked down nearly to the water's edge where the sand was harder and easy to walk on.

For the first time she wondered if she would feel lonely living here by herself. She had told Belinda that it wasn't a problem, but she had never lived on her own before. Ah well, she would soon find out what it felt like. Tomorrow would be spent looking over the cottages she hadn't yet seen. Belinda had promised to show her over them after breakfast and explain what was involved with the cleaning.

She could almost hear Annabel's voice in her head . . . *now's the chance to visit the old man, Taryn Curnow.* But she had no transport of her own. It was too late in the day to go into town now and make enquiries about public transport at the Tourist Office, but she would do so as soon as she had the chance.

*   *   *

Madrenna was on a bus route. That much Carina learned from the bus timetable in the information pack in Thrift Cottage, which she was studying while waiting for the Blackett family to arrive.

The name sprang up at her immediately and she rummaged in her pocket for a pad and biro to write the bus times down. Next, she flipped through the town brochure that described everything that went on locally in glorious Technicolor. Golden beaches, azure sea, emerald headlands, surfing, of course, nearby golf courses, tourist parks, hotels, apartments . . . wow! Why would anyone ever want to spend holidays anywhere else with all this, and more, on offer down here? Smiling, she glanced out of the window at the grey sky. Ah well, anyone could dream.

The pages at the back of the tourist information pack were devoted to adverts for accommodation in guesthouses and two or three residential and nursing homes. Suddenly alert, Carina turned the page and saw a photo of Madrenna Nursing Home, with a phone number. She hadn't expected an opportunity like this.

She pulled out her mobile. No signal here at Thrift Cottage. Wouldn't you just know it? Ten minutes had passed since the Blackett family had alerted her of their imminent arrival. Too much to risk by going outside to the nearest point she could pick up a signal.

Ah, there were signs of their arrival now. A car had pulled up outside and Carina rushed to open the door, a welcoming smile on her face. Yesterday, the people had been delighted to find someone waiting to greet them and show them round. Today, the elderly man emerging from the driving seat glowered at her.

'Mr Blackett?' Carina said, moving forward.

'The directions were abysmal,' he said, ignoring her out-stretched hand. 'How d'you expect anyone to get here with information like that?'

'Now Dad,' said a younger woman, scrambling out of the back seat with a toddler in her arms. 'Let's just get inside. Time enough to start your grumbling when we've got settled.'

The other two members of the party were a young couple, entwined and loving, who stood to one side while Mr Blackett heaved suitcases and rucksacks out of the car and staggered with them to the door. Carina rushed to help. 'Get out of my way,' he barked, red-faced.

Surprised, she kept back, turning to the young woman, who shrugged as she followed her father inside. 'I'm Ginny Fellows,' she said, 'and this is Toby.'

'Toby?' said Carina doubtfully. 'I don't think we knew about him coming.'

'Couldn't leave him at home, could I?'

Carina bit her lip, considering. Toby looked far to young to be sleeping in a single bed and Belinda hadn't said anything about providing a cot.

Oh dear. Problem number one. Problem number two became apparent when the key to the patio door was missing.

'I'll check on that and get back to you,' Carina said.

'And the cot and the high chair?' Ginny said.

'Those as well.' Carina hoped she sounded more positive than she felt.

She ran back to *Spray Point* and picked up the phone, willing Belinda to answer. It wouldn't take long to get the cot and high chair to Thrift Cottage in the van if she was available to do it.

The ringing tone came to an end. A message on the answerphone was the only option, but it was hardly satisfactory. Carina replaced the receiver thoughtfully. She had visions of Mr Blackett attacking the glass in the patio doors with a sledgehammer if she

43

didn't do something quickly.

The phone rang and she snatched up the receiver. Oh no. A call from the other family, as instructed, to say they had just reached Penwick. Luckily, the cottage they were to have for the week was next door to Thrift Cottage, which was just as well in the circumstances.

She ran back, hoping to find the occupants of Thrift Cottage enjoying a cup of tea with young Toby playing with his toys on the rug. No such luck.

'This isn't good enough,' Mr Blackett said, meeting her at the door. 'We're paying enough for the place. We expect it to be properly equipped.

'And it will be as soon as I can contact the owner.'

He snorted.

'Leave her alone, Dad,' Ginny said. She shifted young Toby from one hip to the other. The young couple seemed to have vanished.

Mr Blackett stumped into the living room and across to the patio door. 'A garden,' they said. 'Useful for sitting out and barbecuing, they said. So how do we do that if we can't get out there? Eh? Tell me that, young lady.'

'There's a shared path at the side between this cottage and the next through the gate,' Carina explained. 'No problem, really.'

Mr Blackett glared at her. 'A shared path. I don't like the sound of that. I don't like your attitude, either. If this is what we're to expect, I've a good mind to get in the car and go straight back home.'

Before he could do anything so drastic, Carina heard another vehicle draw up outside and with relief she went to investigate.

'Now where are you going?' Mr Blackett shouted. 'I demand you come back and sort us out before dealing with anyone else. We were here first.'

'I'll be with you in a moment, Mr Blackett,' Carina said with as much patience as she could muster.

The newly arrived holidaymakers were, mercifully, smiling at her as they struggled out of their car clutching bags and jackets.

'Mr and Mrs Ashley? I'm Carina Curnow. I hope you had a good journey?'

'Perfect, didn't we love?' the young man said, turning to his wife. 'We're Jon and Maria and these two urchins are our twins, James and Rosie.'

Carina smiled at the children. 'Hello, you two. Shall I show you where you'll be sleeping?'

There was no need. The children, squealing with excitement, had already discovered their room on the ground floor. Their parents were equally pleased with all she had to show them. Why couldn't everyone be like the Ashleys? Carina thought with feeling.

Back at Thrift Cottage, she found that

Ginny had filled the kettle and plugged it in. Her father, with his young grandson under one arm, was gazing moodily at the washing machine. Surely he hadn't had time to load in his dirty washing, only to find the machine had taken against him? Carina explained she would make enquiries about the missing key, the cot and high chair, and be back with them all very soon. An optimistic assumption on her part, but what else was she to do?

Only one thing as it turned out, cart the furniture by hand from Spray Point to Thrift Cottage as best she could.

With difficulty, she lugged it out of the front door and stacked it by the wall. The high chair would be relatively easy and she would do that first. The distance between Spray Point and Thrift Cottage hadn't seemed great in the van but on foot, and carrying an unwieldy cargo, it was a different matter.

Arriving at the cottage, hot and exhausted, she was glad to see that Toby was now toddling about on the grass in the back garden watched by the young couple who were perched side by side on the wooden picnic bench. She was even more surprised to see that the patio door was wide open.

'What idiot leaves the place unlocked?' Mr Blackett said when he saw Carina. 'I shall have something to say to the Tourist Board about this. Just see if I don't.'

'I'll go and get the cot now,' Carina said. 'I

won't be long.'

This time, she noticed a public pathway that seemed like a short cut and she took it, pleased with her discovery. All the same, the cot, a heavy wooden one that thankfully folded up, was a totally different proposition from the high chair. She tried Belinda again on her home phone and then on her mobile, with no result. Where was the woman when she was needed?

She looked despairingly at the folded cot. She would only be able to manage to carry the frame, so another journey back and forth would be necessary for the rest of it. And what about the bedding? She'd think about that later.

Down the slope she went, lugging the wooden frame with her, and stopped at the bottom to get her breath before negotiating the rutted road that turned into the tarmacked one lined on one side by the parked vehicles of the surfers. She had only gone a short distance when a voice hailed her from the open back of a van.

'Hi, there. Want any help with that?'

She dumped her cargo on the ground and supported it with her body.

The owner of the voice jumped down and she saw that he was the fair-haired surfer she had almost collided with on the steps to the beach yesterday afternoon. Instead of a wetsuit, he was now wearing long khaki shorts and a black T-shirt.

'Are you taking up furniture moving as a career?' he said, his voice full of amusement. 'So where are you taking this? Want a lift?'

She let out a sigh of relief. 'That would be great. It has to go to a cottage in Loveday Place. D'you know it? And . . .' she hesitated, not knowing if she had the nerve to ask another favour, but the kindness in the surfer's smiled decided her. 'There's more I couldn't carry with this, the cot mattress and the base and the bedding. D'you think you could transport those, too?'

'Sure. Here, give me that,' and he heaved the cot into the back of the van as she raced back to Spray Point.

She was back within minutes clutching the rest of the cot and its accompanying duvet set and pillows, which she had found on the clothes airer in the hall.

'Jump in the front then,' the surfer said. 'The name's Jamie Trent. And yours?'

She told him as they set off. 'So you're a surfer, Jamie?'

'You could say that. I work at the surf school, but this is my afternoon off. I like to do a bit of surfing on this side of the bay sometimes.'

'Lucky for me that I ran into you.'

'Sure is. That was a hefty load you were carrying.'

'I've got a job as a cleaner and organiser

with some holiday letting people. I only arrived yesterday, so I'm pretty green. Belinda said . . .'

He braked suddenly to avoid a stray dog. 'Not Belinda Penberthy?'

'You know her?'

'Who doesn't round here? I don't envy you working for the Penberthys.'

'You don't?'

'It's a wonder she can keep the business going the way she refuses to employ enough staff.' Jamie grinned. 'So Belinda's the one making you cart this stuff about? That figures.'

Carina wished she had kept quiet. Kind as this guy Jamie was, she felt disloyal talking about her employer behind her back. And then she felt even worse. They were arriving at Loveday Place now. And there, in the doorway of Thrift Cottage, stood Belinda.

BELINDA PROVES DIFFICULT

As Jamie drew to a halt, Carina sprang out of the van. 'We've collected the cot and bedding,' she told Belinda. 'Jamie here was kind enough to transport it for me.'

'So I see,' said Belinda, and by the expression on her face, she didn't seem pleased. 'I wish you had thought of contacting me before you started heaving it from one

49

place to another.'

Carina looked at her in surprise. Surely Belinda realised that the Blackett family included a young child who needed somewhere to sleep? If she didn't, then the grandfather would surely have pointed it out.

'I left messages on your answer phone and voice mail,' said Carina. 'I thought the best thing to do was to collect the items myself.' She might just as well not have spoken, for all the notice Belinda took.

Feeling awkward, Carina helped Jamie unload the cot and together they carried it into the cottage, Belinda standing to one side.

'D'you think you could possibly take it upstairs for me?' asked Ginny tentatively.

'Sure,' said Jamie.

Carina threw Ginny a sympathetic glance as she heard Mr Blackett on the landing barking orders.

Belinda asked if there was anything else the clients needed. 'No, that's lovely,' Ginny said. 'I'm so grateful.'

'And so she should be,' said Belinda grimly, when they got outside. 'There was no request for a cot and high chair on the booking form. They're lucky to get them.'

'There would have been ructions if they hadn't,' Jamie muttered. 'I met Mr Blackett upstairs when I was delivering the cot. Some holiday this is going to be for that poor young woman.'

'You've been great,' Carina whispered. 'I couldn't have managed without you.'

'Are you free later? There's a barbecue down on the beach. Come and join us if you like.'

'She won't like,' said Belinda, overhearing. 'I'm taking you out in the van this evening, Carina. See how you shape up.'

'As a driver?'

'What else? You can't manage without transport and you've none of your own.'

Carina knew that Belinda was right. She looked at Jamie apologetically. 'Perhaps another time?'

'I'm off upcountry tomorrow for a while. But Zena will be here.'

'Zena?'

He ran his hand through his blond hair. 'A pal of mine. She'll look after you.'

Carina smiled, but was inwardly disappointed. She quite liked Jamie. It would have been nice to spend an evening getting to know the other people who lived here.

She had to admit that being here, in a new place, on her own, was beginning to feel a bit lonely.

The van was an automatic and once Carina had got used to the controls, she found it easier to cope with than she had feared. She drove through the narrow streets of the town with care, Belinda pointing out how much busier it would become as the season went on. She wanted Carina to familiarise herself with the place so she didn't sound ignorant when answering questions about the locality.

'Study the brochures,' Belinda said, as Carina drove up the lane back to Spray Point. 'You'll find a pile of them somewhere in the kitchen.'

Carina manoeuvred the van up the steep slope to the parking place and applied the handbrake.

'Well done,' said Belinda gruffly. 'You'll do.'

Carina flushed at the unexpected praise.

'Tomorrow, I'll need an inventory done of everything in here,' Belinda said, as they emerged into the breezy air. 'You have computer skills, I believe? There's one installed in the conservatory under some of that paper on the table. Windows XP. Can you cope with that?'

'I think so,' Carina answered. 'Is there a password?'

Belinda told her what it was.

'So do you want me to open a folder and make a list of what's in here?' Carina said.

Belinda nodded. 'And do a print-out. And when you've done that, there's shopping you need to do for the properties. You might clear a space somewhere to store what you buy. Oh, and be sure to keep accounts. There's money

52

in the tin in the kitchen cupboard, but keep the receipts. As I told you, we equip our places with the obvious things, a welcome tray of tea, coffee, and sugar. And we leave milk and orange juice in the fridge for when guests arrive, but you won't need to purchase those until the day before. And don't forget the soap and toothpaste.'

'I won't,' said Carina, making mental notes.

'Oh, and shower gel and a few other things. We need a good supply of washing powder, too. Don't forget that. You'll launder the bedding over here, but check the machines are working in the apartment and cottages. And make sure there are some dishwasher tablets in the cupboard under the sinks.'

'I'll do that,' said Carina.

'I'll leave you then.'

'Would you like me to drive you home?'

'That won't be necessary. If you need practice driving the van on your own to build your confidence, feel free to go off somewhere in your free time.'

Free time? It sounded as if there would be precious little of that. But what a golden opportunity!

Pulling out her mobile, Carina dialled the number of Madrenna Nursing Home. 'I phoned the other day about a Mr Curnow, who I believe is with you,' she said, when the call was answered.

'Just a moment please. Who is calling?'

'I'm Carina Curnow.'

'A relative?'

'Well, no. Or, that is, maybe. I don't know. I'm wondering if . . . I mean, I . . .'

'Well, dear, either you are or you aren't. And if you're not, I am afraid I can't give out information about any of our residents.' The phone clicked off.

Carina couldn't really blame the woman. She knew she must have sounded like some mad person. But how was she ever to find out about Taryn Curnow? Turning up on the doorstep wouldn't be any good, she reasoned. They'd probably call the police and have me arrested as some sort of stalker of the elderly.

Disappointed, she went indoors.

If she worked hard now, and again tomorrow morning, she would have the afternoon free to visit Poltizzy and maybe find the house where her father had grown up. Someone there might be able to tell her more about the Curnow family and about the old man at Madrenna Nursing Home.

Later, exhausted and hungry, Carina pulled the curtains across the windows of the living-room, shutting out the dark and the distant glow from the fire that had been lit on the beach. For a moment she had considered joining the crowd down there, but then thought better of it. She was better off here, getting on with things at Spray Point, so she could have some free time tomorrow before Belinda had a chance to land her with something else that needed doing.

She sighed as she went into the kitchen to see what she could find in the freezer. A pizza would do nicely. Taking one out, she defrosted it in the microwave, turned on the oven and then sat down at the table to wait until it was cooked. The window in here was curtainless and her reflection stared back at her. True, the window faced a blank wall, but it felt eerie knowing that anyone could creep up the side of the bungalow and peer in.

She shivered. She would give anything to see Sadie's kind face smiling at her now. Annabel's, too, and her friends at work.

Suddenly she was no longer hungry. The darkness outside seemed oppressive and worrying. She got up from the table to turn off the oven, wishing she were anywhere but here. She had a sudden vision of the kitchen at home, cosy and warm, with Sadie's collection of bird prints on the wall. Her longing to be there was like an ache. What was she doing here, alone, in this untidy, crowded bungalow, starting a job that seemed more like hard slog than anything else? It was crazy.

For a moment, she stood there fighting a rising panic and then she sat down again. She had chosen to come here of her own free will and it was only her second day. Things would get better; they had to. She would phone Annabel for a long talk about nothing in particular and pretend her friend was in the next room. And after that, cheered up, she would phone Sadie.

She leaned over to reach the switch for the oven and turned it back on.

*   *   *

'Oh dear,' Sadie said.

'What's wrong?' Rob said, shaking out the tea towel and hanging it on its rail.

'That was Carina.'

'And?'

'She says she's enjoying herself down there, working hard and seeing people into the accommodation.'

'So what's the problem?'

His mother shrugged as she emptied the bowl of washing up water. 'There isn't one, I suppose.'

'So what then?'

Sadie sighed. 'I worry about her, that's all.'

'You still want her under your wing, so you can organise her life?'

'Organise?' said Sadie in indignation. 'I do not.' She frowned. 'It's just that I have a feeling something's not right. She hasn't seen that old man yet, the one in the nursing home. Taryn Curnow's his name. It would mean so much to her to know she had some family.'

'We're her family. Doesn't it hurt you that she thinks we're not good enough?'

'It's not like that, Rob. Do try to understand. I know full well why she's doing it. I don't want her to get hurt, that's all.'

'And what about you getting hurt?'

Sadie straightened her back and smiled at her son.

'We have to set Carina free. This is something she has to do.'

'At the expense of your happiness?'

'We all have to make our own way in life and do what feels right for us.'

Rob picked up on the brief note of sadness in his mother's voice. Carina seemed to have matured a lot in the three years since he'd left, but she was still his mother's baby, the child she had taken into their home. It was hard for Mum.

'Just say the word and I'll drop you off at work tomorrow and then drive down and check on Carina for you,' he said. 'How's that for an idea?'

'All that way and back in a day?'

'No problem. And I can bring her back with me if she really hates it down there. What do you say?'

Sadie shook her head. 'Let's just see how it goes, shall we? At least give her a chance to visit the old man, Taryn Curnow, in the nursing home down there.'

'Taryn.' Rob said. 'What sort of a name's that? I'm glad you had more sense than to land me with something like that.'

Sadie reached up to put the dry dinner plates on the shelf. 'Your father wanted to call you Damien,' she grinned.

'Just as well he didn't!'

'Robert was my father's name,' Sadie explained. 'Now let's go into the living-room and I'll show you the information that's come about my bird-watching week.'

Rob gave his mother a hug, glad she had something else to think about. She deserved a bit of *me* time, and he would see that she got it.

Next morning, Carina felt better. She lay in bed for a while, listening to the sound of the sea, then she threw the covers back and padded across to the window. The rising sun was sending streams of glorious gold across the water and the sky was a rosy hue. The breakers surged in from the ocean and broke in great bursts of foam on the shore. And of course, early as it was, the surfers were out.

She watched for a moment, imagining their exhilaration as they rode the waves. It must feel wonderful.

She breakfasted on cereal and toast and then set about clearing the kitchen of anything that should have a home elsewhere. Today, the stocktaking didn't seem such a daunting task, and starting this early gave her a virtuous glow.

She broke off at mid-morning for a quick coffee followed by an expedition to the supermarket in town to fulfil Belinda's orders. Glad that at least that was done, she continued with her stocktaking list, pleased that she seemed to be getting on so well.

She was so engrossed she didn't hear Belinda arrive and was startled to see her standing in the doorway.

'Nearly complete?' Belinda said.

'Not yet,' said Carina rising from her seat at the computer. 'I've listed all the bedding and most of the bath towels and hand towels. When I've cleared in here, I'll stack them in piles out of the way. I haven't attempted to sort out the other bedrooms yet, or the things in the bathroom, but I'll make a start on that this evening.'

'Why not this afternoon?'

'I have something to do this afternoon.'

Belinda looked at her through narrowed eyes. 'May I ask what?'

Carina hesitated. It wouldn't do to sound rude, but this wasn't really Belinda's business. 'I've been working hard since early this morning, so I thought I'm due some time off.'

'You're not planning to fraternise with that young fellow you were with yesterday?'

'I have no other plans than to go out by

myself,' Carina said.

The older woman looked none too pleased. 'I don't know,' she said. 'The sooner this job is completed, the better. You'll be busy on Tuesday picking up some things on order from Truro and then cleaning out the shed at the back here for extra storage space.'

'I need a few hours off each day, too,' said Carina. 'This afternoon is the most convenient for me.'

'But not for me,' said Belinda.

'I shall continue with the stocktaking this evening,' Carina said firmly. 'I'll go on into the night if necessary, but I need some time off now. It seems perfectly in order to me.'

'Oh it does, does it?'

Carina was determined not to give in. She waited a moment and then said, 'I'm sorry, Belinda, but I must insist on something that seems perfectly fair.'

'Very well then,' Belinda said grudgingly. 'But see that you make up for it later.'

*   *   *

After a quick sandwich lunch, Carina set off for Poltizzy, feeling excitement bubble up inside her as she drove past Madrenna Nursing Home on the bend in the narrow lane. Ahead of her was the village of Poltizzy and she drew up outside the Post Office and jumped out of the van.

'Poltizzy House, m'dear?' said the elderly man behind the counter. 'Ah yes, go right on through the village till you come to the crossroads. Turn left there and go on up the hill and you'll see the drive straight ahead. The house is down-along behind the trees. You can't miss it.'

The last thing Carina wanted was to drive up to the front of the house in Belinda's van, but parking near the entrance wasn't an option because the lane was narrow, high-banked and winding. So she turned carefully in the open gateway and returned the way she had come. She found a parking space near the old school and walked up to Poltizzy House. She went in through the open gates, imagining her father as a young boy running and playing here in these lovely tree-dotted grounds. What a place to grow up!

She wished he had told her about it, young as she was. But his mind had obviously been on other things than his young, motherless daughter, who had needed him so badly. Carina knew that what she saw as her father's rejection of her had coloured her life, and her sense of loss had never quite gone away.

Now, she rounded the bend in the drive and stopped in delight. Below her, the large creeper-covered building looked welcoming.

61

The house was built of granite and roofed with grey slate and seemed as if it had been here forever, sunk into the ground from where its stone came.

A car horn tooted and she jumped to one side in alarm. Awkward at being caught in the grounds of the house, Carina was ready with her explanation and went towards the open window of the vehicle, smiling.

The grey Mercedes skidded to a halt and the male driver in dark suit and sunglasses glared at her. 'I must ask you to leave at once, Miss Curnow,' he said.

She opened her mouth to speak and then shut it again.

'You *are* Miss Curnow?'

She nodded.

'You're not welcome here. Do you understand?'

She found herself nodding again. Then, ashamed of her capitulation when she had no idea what this was about, she stared back at him. 'But why?'

'My solicitor will be informed. You will hear from him in due course.' The driver released the handbrake and moved off.

She stared after him, open-mouthed. This man knew who she was. Not only that, he knew exactly where she was living. Suddenly she thought of the uncurtained window at Spray Point that had so alarmed her last night. Her fears had maybe been not so foolish after all.

CARINA MAKES A FRIEND

Carina got herself back to the parked van, unlocked the door and clambered inside, clasping her trembling hands in her lap. Who was that man? And how did he know her name? There were things going on here she didn't understand or care much for.

She drove back to Spray Point, her mind still whirling.

That horrible man had assumed she was up to no good without even giving her a chance to explain.

What's more, he seemed to have expected her to turn up in the drive of Poltizzy House.

After a while, she became conscious that she was being followed. A motorbike, careful not to overtake, slowed down each time she did and kept at the same distance behind her. Surely the man she had encountered hadn't swapped from a Mercedes to a bike in seconds, with a swift change of clothes from dark suit to leathers kept behind a handy rhododendron for just such an occasion?

Carina slowed down at the roundabout, hoping the motorbike would veer off to the right. No such luck. She bit her lip as the van juddered up the rough road to Spray Point, still closely tailed. Her mouth was dry as she turned into the steep drive and the motorbike drew up behind her.

Before her courage deserted her, she took a deep breath and sprang out to face her pursuer. The rider hoisted the bike on to its stand and the helmet was whipped off.

Carina, staring, saw a girl, with straight black hair and brown eyes. 'Who are you?' she demanded.

'Didn't startle you, did I?' the girl said.

'What's the big idea?'

'I'm Zena.'

'Zena? Oh, *Zena.*' Carina felt weak with relief and leaned against the car. 'Jamie's friend? But why are you following me?'

'Jamie asked me to look out for you and I know the Penberthy van only too well. I used to drive it myself. When I saw you at the Poltizzy turn it seemed a good idea to follow you back. So here I am.'

'A strange way of befriending me, frightening me to death.' Carina took several deep breaths.

'I didn't think. Sorry.'

'It's okay. I probably overreacted.'

'Come on then, what are you waiting for?' Zena marched on ahead up the steps to the front door, swinging her helmet in one hand. Inside, she looked at the folded beds stacked against the wall and the dustbin liners full of the items needed for the properties and wrinkled her nose. 'It's even worse than when I worked here. The place needs knocking down.

And look at all this stuff. I heard she'd got more places that need kitting out, but even so . . .'

'*You* worked for Belinda?'

'I did a temporary job last year in the height of the season to earn some cash before I started work at the Comprehensive.'

'You're a teacher?'

Zena nodded. 'Supply work. I'm looking round for something else now. Working for Belinda didn't last long. I got the push for skiving off one afternoon. How come you've been allowed time off already?'

Carina shuddered.

Zena looked at her closely. 'Are you all right?'

'Why d'you ask?'

'You don't look it.'

'I had a bit of a shock back there at Poltizzy, that's all.' Carina leaned on the bed frame against the wall and ran her hand over her face.

'Come on, let's find you a seat.' Zena opened the living room door, took one look inside and slammed the door shut again. 'Any space in the kitchen?'

Carina took a deep restorative breath. 'Yes, there is. Coffee?'

Zena's dark eyes lit up as she smiled. 'Lead on.'

At least the kitchen was tidy and they could sit down at the table without having to move

65

great piles of bedding and towels. Carina plugged in the kettle and found a packet of biscuits. She made the coffee and carried the mugs to the table.

'So what's been happening to shock you so?' said Zena, as she unzipped her leather jacket and pulled it off.

Carina was feeling better already and could feel the colour returning to her cheeks. 'I'm sorry I snapped at you, Zena,' she said. 'It's just that, well, I was attacked verbally by someone I met and I don't know why, or indeed, who he was.'

'Did you give as good as you got?'

To her shame, Carina remembered that she hadn't exactly stood up for herself 'I was trespassing,' she said, by way of an explanation. 'I felt in the wrong.'

'Where was this?'

'Not far from where you first saw me.'

Zena said nothing else for a moment and Carina studied the dark head held slightly to one side.

'So how did you manage to get the afternoon free?' Zena said at last.

'I've been working all hours since I got here yesterday,' Carina said. 'I was exhausted. I thought I was due some time off and told Belinda so.'

'And she agreed? Wow! You must have stood your ground well.'

'But I let myself be browbeaten back there

at Poltizzy House.'

'Poltizzy House? What were you doing there?'

'My father was born there,' Carina said. It felt good saying it out loud.

She opened a packet of biscuits and offered one to Zena. 'I just thought I'd take a look at it this afternoon, that's all, see where he grew up. I was sure I'd be able to see it from the road, but the trees are in the way.'

'Blocking the view,' Zena agreed.

'This car came sweeping down the drive. A Mercedes. I'd only gone a little way inside the gates, just far enough to see the house.'

'Don't tell me. A dark-haired chap, smartly dressed? Frowning and short-tempered?'

Carina was surprised. 'You know him?'

'I've met him a few times. Horrible man, Marcus Trent. Jamie's utterly different. As nice as they come.'

'So Jamie is connected with that dreadful man?'

Zena helped herself to a biscuit. 'His brother. You'd hardly believe it, would you?'

'And they live at Poltizzy House?'

'Their mother lives there. She moved in when Jamie's father was too ill to cope on his own. Jamie's got a flat in town and Marcus lives over Kiltennie way.'

Carina slowly stirred her coffee. 'So why didn't Marcus assume I was visiting his mother? And why did he threaten me with a

67

solicitor's letter if I didn't keep away?'

Zena sat up straight. 'He *threatened* you? I don't believe it. That's crazy even for Marcus.'

'A bit scary, don't you agree?'

'Money, that's what it is, money,' Zena said. 'Everything's always down to money with Marcus.'

'Well, I don't know what he thinks I've got to do with any money. Someone in the village told me about old Mr Curnow who lived at Poltizzy House. I just thought it was interesting, because when we were checking my surname on the 1901 census, it came up with Vyvyan Curnow of Poltizzy House.'

Zena was wide-eyed with interest. 'So your name's Curnow?'

Carina nodded. 'I haven't any relations, so it was wonderful to find someone who might be family, as you can imagine. And it seemed too good to be true when I heard about this job and was offered it.'

'So you've been doing some research into your family?'

Carina shook her head. 'No point, really.' She started to explain about her parents' lack of siblings, but Zena wasn't listening. 'There's every point,' she said. 'If you're down here slaving for Belinda, you must want to find out something. Marcus might have a shock coming to him.' She sounded triumphant, as if this thought had made her day.

'So where do you fit in, Zena?' Carina said.

'Have you lived round here for long?'

'Only since last summer when I started to work for Belinda. Then I met Jamie. He got me into surfing and I decided not to go back home to Nottingham. Now I work part time at the local supermarket. For the moment, anyway.'

'Are you and Jamie . . . ?'

Zena shook her head. 'To tell you the truth, I fell for Marcus at one point, more fool me. But nothing came of that.'

'I see,' Carina said, but she didn't really. Jamie seemed far the nicer of the two. She smiled as she thought of his kind face and the way his eyes twinkled when he looked at her. She liked the way he smiled, too, starting slowly, as if he wasn't quite sure of the reaction, and then developing into a huge grin. She'd thought of him a lot since yesterday afternoon. She stared dreamily into her coffee, wondering when she would see him again.

Zena left, roaring off on her motorbike after promising to be in touch during the next day or two. Carina watched until she reached the road, zoomed past the parked vehicles and disappeared over the brow of the hill. With a last look at the black specks of the surfers riding the waves, she went back indoors.

The place felt lonely without Zena's
69

presence but there was a lot for her to think about. Poltizzy House for one, that lovely building she had glimpsed only briefly and that had been Dad's home when he was young. Had it been a wrench to leave it? She would never know, as she wouldn't a lot of other things, either.

But she knew about Taryn Curnow, the old man in the nursing home.

Musing on this, she decided to finish her inventory before making preparations for an early meal. After that, she would start clearing out the shed, so that a lot of the stuff could be stored neatly, ready for when it was required.

An image of Jamie Trent's slow smile filled Carina's mind as she switched on the computer and got her stock-taking file up on screen. She added the number of orange bath towels she had counted earlier and then entered the number of green ones. Having this list would prove to be useful in the future but getting it all sorted out and checked was boring in the extreme. Never mind, it would soon be done.

The phone rang in the living room.

'Sadie!' she said with pleasure.

There was so much to tell her, but some instinct made Carina omit any mention of Marcus Trent.

'I've made a friend,' she said.

'Already?' Sadie sounded pleased.

'Zena's her name. She rides a motorbike.

70

And I've been over to Poltizzy again. Mr Curnow still can't have visitors, but I hope to be in contact soon.'

'We were worried about you, Carina, after your last phone call. You sounded so down. Rob was all for coming down to see for himself and to bring you home.'

Carina was horrified. 'Oh no! I'm fine! Really I am.'

'I can tell you are now,' said Sadie, a smile in her voice.

'This is a gorgeous place,' Carina told her. 'You should see the view. And the beach is fantastic. I might even think of having surfing lessons one day.'

'Rob would love to do that. Being cooped up here in Bristol isn't his scene.'

Carina gave a little sigh. Rob again. Better not mention Jamie, or Sadie would have her son down here like a shot, booking into one of the local bed and breakfasts for the season. Or, worse still, expecting to be put up at Spray Point. She stared in dismay at the curtains moving slightly in the breeze and at the view of the sea beyond. She could see Rob here quite easily, making himself at home without the slightest doubt that he would be welcome anywhere he chose to show up.

'So what have you been up to, Sadie?' she said.

For the rest of the phone-call they talked of a forthcoming bird-watching holiday Sadie had booked on the Exe estuary in Devon.

*   *   *

Carina worked hard until she had transferred the list of all the information she had gathered into the computer.

'Shed, here I come,' she said, leaning back and stretching when the screen was blank once more. She allowed herself a few minutes rest before going to change into her oldest jeans and a sagging jersey.

A voice hailed her as she went outside. 'Carina!'

Carina looked up and her heart leapt.

'Jamie!'

He came bounding up the steps looking smarter than she had seen him before, in a light jacket and trousers, the shade of blue of his shirt matching his eyes. 'I'm on my way to see a neighbour of yours. Tim Denton. Lives up here somewhere. Know him'?'

She shook her head, conscious of her appearance.

'Nor me. I need to talk to him, find out a few things.'

'I'm just about to start clearing out the shed,' she said, in case he thought she always dressed like this.

He looked interested. 'For extra storage? Can I have a look?'

He stood back as she opened the shed door

to reveal a stack of bin liners filled with rubbish and grey with dust.

'The shed's dry enough,' said Jamie, stepping inside.

'And someone's put up those shelves,' Carina added. 'Perfect for storing all the smaller items I'll need for kitting out the properties.'

'Useful,' said Jamie. 'And so's that wooden work bench.'

'I'll stack bigger stuff on that, bath sheets and towels.'

'You've got it all thought out.'

'It needs a good clean out, that's all, and then I'll be able to see what I want at a glance. So much easier.'

'I'll help you get the bags outside.'

'Dressed like that?'

Jamie looked down at his smart clothes. 'Maybe not. Anyway, I'll have to go. I couldn't resist calling out to you when I saw you.'

Carina shut the shed door behind them. 'A job for tomorrow, this. Now I've seen what's what, I'm happier about it.'

They began to walk to the front of the bungalow.

'I saw your brother today,' she said by way of conversation and, she admitted to herself, to gauge his reaction.

Jamie frowned. 'Marcus? I thought he was abroad. Speak to you, did he?'

She shook her head. Somehow, she didn't

73

want Jamie to know about her conversation with Marcus. 'It was only a brief glance,' she lied. 'But Zena said it was him.'

A strange expression flickered across Jamie's face. 'So you've met Zena, too?'

'She's nice. I like meeting people.'

He nodded. 'Me too. And the chap I'm meeting was expecting me ten minutes ago.'

Out at sea, dusk was beginning to haze the horizon. An early night again tonight, Carina thought, as she watched Jamie go. Oh well, she would start work out here in the fresh air of early morning.

A WONDERFUL DISCOVERY

Sending a get-well card to the old gentleman, Taryn Curnow, in the nursing home, was such an obvious thing to do that Carina wondered why it hadn't occurred to her before. Since she couldn't visit him, this was as good a way as any of introducing herself and letting him know she wished him well.

In the meantime, though, there was a lot to do. Cleaning out the shed took longer than she had anticipated and she didn't start moving things into it until after lunch. Then, needing a break from all the heaving and carrying, she showered and changed into clean clothes before setting off on foot for town. The cars and vans parked alongside the road overlooking the bay weren't so numerous today, but the sea was still dotted with surfers. On her return, she paused for a while to watch them.

If only she had more free time, she could go down to the beach and book in for some surfing lessons. Never mind. Maybe when she got used to the work schedule everything would seem as easy as she had led Sadie to believe, and she would have some time to herself.

By Thursday evening, the shed was filled to capacity with everything labelled and easy to locate and Spray Point was clean and tidy. Belinda, visiting to see how Carina was getting on, was impressed.

'Two families are going out from the apartments tomorrow,' she told Carina when they were in the kitchen drinking coffee, 'and we've got one family coming in. You've got the list for the next two days?'

'It's here,' Carina said opening the cupboard by the door to show her.

Belinda nodded in approval when she saw the neatly-typed list Sellotaped to the inside of the cupboard door. 'We need more bookings to keep going. of course, but it should pick up.

'You'll be able to cope with it all?'

'I think so, yes,' Carina said. 'But it might be a bit tricky seeing more than one family in at a time, especially if one is in a cottage and the other is in the apartments.'

'Then you'll just have to work things out,' Belinda said briskly, as she stood up to go.

*   *   *

'She overworks you,' said Jamie. 'You should make a stand.'

Carina looked at him standing there on the path above the beach looking so vigorous and healthy in his shorts and sleeveless shirt, that he might have stepped straight out of an advert for a fitness magazine. His fair hair seemed to glisten in the evening sunshine.

She smiled. 'Easy for you to say, but where else would I find another job down here with accommodation I can afford?'

He grinned. 'Fancy walking to the top of Crowen Head?'

'Why not?' she said. 'It's a perfect evening and I need a break' She could relax for a while now that the Friday family had settled in.

'I've come out to clear my head, too,' Jamie said. 'I've got a big new project on. I'm boring everyone with talking about my new plans and I need a new sounding board.'

Carina laughed as they began to climb the path to the top of the grassy hill. 'Try me, then,' she said.

'Ever heard of coasteering?'

'Coasteering?'

'A new thing; the name, anyway. I've been

doing it since I was a kid and so have loads of others round here. But now it's official, with a proper name, and I want to get in on it and start up my own business before anyone else gets the same idea.'

'So what is it?'

They had reached the top of the hill now where a small white building stood. It looked interesting but Carina was too intrigued by what Jamie was telling her to do anything else but sit down beside him on the seat outside to regain her breath from the climb.

'It's the in-thing at the moment, coasteering. We're calling the company *Leapaway*. A good name, don't you think?' Jamie said.

'*Leapaway*,' Carina said reflectively. 'An action word. I like it.' He looked pleased. 'I thought of the name suddenly in the middle of the night. We think it sounds good.'

'We?'

'There are one or two people who might be interested in joining me. Between us, we've got a lot of the equipment already, wet suits, buoyancy aids and helmets, that sort of thing.'

'And what does coasteering involve?'

'Basically, it's a walk-jump-swim-climb experience round the coastline, mainly at low tide.'

'But isn't it dangerous?'

'Not when you know what you're doing, are properly equipped and have expert instructors. And the safety precautions are stringent, believe me. Myself and the others have got a couple of vans between us and they'll do to set up in initially. Later, we'll try to rent or buy a building like the old salt house down by the harbour.

'Coasteering will catch on, you'll see. My brother thinks so, too, because he's investing money in us.' Jamie looked out to sea before asking, 'Have you been down to the harbour yet?'

'I didn't know there was one.'

He laughed and put his arm around her in a perfectly natural way, it seemed to Carina. 'Don't know much about the area, do you?' he said.

'Give me a chance. I haven't been here five minutes,' she retorted. She liked being close to him, and she liked the feel of his arm on her shoulder. She felt carefree, suddenly, and young.

'You need someone to show you around if Belinda allows you any more time off,' Jamie said. 'How about coming to the Saturday barbecue on the beach, since you couldn't make it last time? Or, better still, we could end up there after going somewhere ourselves. *The Surge and Swell* by the harbour wall is a great place.'

'Sounds good,' Carina said.

'See you there tomorrow, then, about eight.' Jamie moved his arm and leaned forward. 'I can tell you more about *Leapaway* then,' he

78

said. 'You're an expert on the computer and we could use some input on that. And we might need to recommend accommodation for some of our clients.'

Carina heard the postman arrive while she was having breakfast a few days later. On the mat was a postcard with a photograph of a large house. Madrenna Nursing Home. She turned it over eagerly to read the spidery handwriting that invited her to visit Mr Curnow on Saturday afternoon between two o'clock and four. Today.

This was it then. Success! Luckily, only one family was scheduled to arrive and the official time for that was four o'clock. She would have her mobile with her just in case they were early.

But this could be her only chance to make contact with Taryn Curnow, and she was going to make the most of it.

*　　　*　　　*

Madrenna Nursing Home looked friendly in the afternoon sunshine and the rhododendrons lining the drive made a welcoming display of colour. This time, Carina drove into the car park. From the few vehicles already there, she seemed to have chosen a quiet time.

She parked in the shade of a willow tree and breathed in the scent of new-mown grass as she opened the van door and got out.

A tall, grey-haired woman greeted her at the front door, so elegantly dressed that Carina was suddenly conscious of her old navy jacket and saggy shoulder bag. She had changed her trainers for sandals, though, and was wearing her best skirt. 'I've come to see Mr Taryn Curnow,' she said. 'I received an invitation to visit him this afternoon.'

She half-expected to be refused admittance, but the woman stood aside for her to enter the deeply carpeted hall. 'Ah yes, Miss Curnow. I'm Marcia Jolliffe, duty matron. Please come this way.'

They found the old man in the conservatory, dozing in a winged armchair by the picture window that overlooked the front lawn. His green sports jacket looked too large for his small frame but the red scarf round his neck gave him a jaunty appearance that belied his age.

'You have a visitor,' Marcia Jolliffe said, smiling kindly at him.

He stirred a little.

'Please don't get up,' Carina said, coming forward to take his hand. It felt thin and papery.

'I've had flu, you know,' he said, in a surprisingly strong voice. 'Better now. Bullied back to health by this woman.'

The matron gave him a fond smile and left them to it.

'Now tell me who you are, my dear,' the old man said. 'It feels good to be intrigued at my age. Curnow, a good Cornish name and the same as mine. Are you Cornish?'

'I was born in Bristol,' Carina said. 'My father's name was Vyvyan James Curnow and he was born at Poltizzy House. That was a long time ago, in 1950. He died in 1992.'

'So . . . another Vyvyan Curnow. Our family tree's full of them.'

'That's why I wondered if there was a family connection.'

'And you'd like there to be?'

Carina leaned forward. 'I would, oh I would.'

His eyes narrowed a little. 'And why is that?'

'I've no relations of my own, you see. It would mean so much to me to find that I had some after all . . .' She broke off, thinking of Sadie and how she had been so loving and kind to her . . . still was, of course. She was lucky.

Taryn Curnow reached forward for the glass of water on the small table nearby and took a few sips.

'I heard you were unwell. I thought I'd like to see you,' Carina went on, taking the glass from his shaking hand and putting it down for him.

'Have you been to Poltizzy House?'

Carina hesitated. 'I just took a look at it from the drive. A lovely place.'

He nodded. 'It is that. And more.'

He was silent for a moment, deep in thought. Carina studied him, taking in the rheumy eyes and thin white hair.

'I was the baby of my family in my generation,' he continued after a while. 'My brother Vyvyan was the eldest, born in 1901. He married late, forty-nine. I was in Africa when his son was born and was there for many years afterwards, so I never met the boy.'

'Your nephew?' said Carina.

'And your father, my dear. Vyvyan James.'

A surge of joy ran through Carina. 'My father,' she whispered.

'Your father, of course. He could be none other, could he, if you are who you say you are.'

'Carina Susan Curnow, daughter of Vyvyan James Curnow and Susan Williams.' It felt good to say the names of her dead parents. It emphasised the fact of their existence.

'You have proof of that?'

'My birth certificate.' She had brought it with her and fumbled for it in her bag. He took it from her and bent his head to read.

'My mother came from Redruth, an only child, too. Her parents are dead now.'

He handed back the certificate and smiled at her so kindly that tears sprang to her eyes.

82

'There certainly doesn't seem to be any doubt, my dear.'

She wiped her eyes, smiling. 'This means so much to me,' she said. 'I'm so glad I've found you.'

There was a stir in the doorway and Carina looked up to see the matron ushering in another visitor. 'Mrs Trent has come to see you,' she said, as she pulled forward a chair for the stout middle-aged lady with her. Then she withdrew silently, closing the door behind her.

'Taryn, how are you?' The woman seated herself heavily, smoothing her navy skirt over her knees and placing the basket she was carrying on the floor at her feet. A bunch of carnations topped some bulky packages. She lifted the flowers out and looked round for somewhere to put them. 'I brought you these.'

'I'll hold them on my lap,' Taryn said. 'Thank you, my dear. Oh, and this young lady is Miss Carina Curnow. A pretty name, don't you think? We've met for the first time today and she's brought something important to show me. Her birth certificate. Mind you keep it safe, my dear.'

Mrs Trent looked appalled as Carina folded the certificate and put it in her bag. 'But who are you?'

'Carina is my great niece, my brother's granddaughter,' the old man said, and looked positively jubilant, Carina thought.

'Marcus won't like this . . .'

'What's it got to do with him?'

Plenty, Carina thought, from the expression on Mrs Trent's face. She rose to go. 'I'll come again next week,' she promised.

'You do that, my dear. I'd like to see you. A pretty young face makes a change from this stuffy lot in here.'

The euphoria from her visit to Madrenna Nursing Home stayed with Carina all the time she was greeting the elderly couple and their two adult daughters and settling them in to the apartment. Their pleasure in it added to her sense of well being and she walked down to the beach with a light heart.

Jamie was waiting for her at the bottom of the steps. 'Change of plan,' he said. 'We're having a meeting about *Leapaway* and you're welcome to attend while the others get cracking with the barbecue. We've had some applications in and need to get a few things sorted out.'

'But won't I be in the way?'

'Not at all. *The Surge and Swell* another night then, all right?'

'All right.'

He took her hand as they walked across the beach. The fire was already lit and several people had gathered round. Two of them called a greeting.

84

'Hi there,' Jamie called back. 'This is Carina.'

No-one seemed to think anything of her gate-crashing and she found herself caught up in the enthusiasm for a project that, if they were to be believed, was about to take off like a rocket. Zena arrived and joined them, adding a few ideas of her own.

'I've put an advert on the Internet for qualified instructors,' someone said. 'Local papers, too, and the dailies. Asking for RYA qualifications, surfing and climbing experience, first aid qualifications, life-saving certificates. All that.'

'Good man,' said Jamie. 'And we've had three applications so far. Is that right?'

'I've already got back to two of them,' said Zena. 'One was no good. The other sounds all right but he'll need to come down to meet us. I said at the weekend. Is that OK?'

'Sure,' said Jamie, then went on, 'So who's going to join me with the first group of clients for a tryout?'

'I will,' said Zena.

Her eyes shone in the light from the fire and as she listened to them making arrangements Carina began to wish she could be one of those taking part in the activities they were so enthusiastic about.

The enticing aroma of sausages and bacon sizzling on the barbecue floated across to them and Carina realised how hungry she was. She and Jamie, plates piled high, sat a little apart from the others, listening to the waves breaking on the sand.

'I picked up on a likely application, too,' he said. 'A chap from your part of the world.'

Carina paused with a hunk of bread halfway to her mouth.

'Says he knows you very well.'

'Not Rob Mason?'

'That's the name. Do you know him well?'

She nodded.

'No good?'

How could she answer that? Rob was exactly the sort of person Jamie was after, except that his holiday would be over soon. She let out a sigh of relief as she remembered that. She was safe, then, because Jamie and his partners needed someone on a more permanent basis.

'He's been setting up an adventure leisure business out in New Zealand,' she explained. 'He's home on holiday and he'll be going back in a couple of weeks. Otherwise, he'd be perfect.'

Jamie looked at her closely. 'I sense a but?'

She shrugged. 'I left Bristol to get away from him.'

'Like that, is it? And you don't want him following you here?' She looked down at the ground. 'Not really.'

'He says his speciality is bungee jumping. Are you sure you got it right about only being

86

around for a short time?'

'I'm sure.'

'Since he's put in an application for the job, it sounds like he might have other ideas now. But, Carina, I don't want you getting upset.'

He was looking at her in such a way that her heart was touched. All the same, if the other applicants turned out to be unsuitable, Jamie might have no choice but to employ Rob.

BELINDA IS NOT IMPRESSED

What I need, thought Carina next morning, is a good night's sleep. I need to wake up refreshed and eager to get on with the cleaning of Thrift Cottage as soon as the Blackett family have vacated it, instead of crawling out of bed bleary-eyed and exhausted because of thinking about Rob. And I forgot to buy a pint of milk yesterday, as well.

Yawning, she pulled open her bedroom curtains and surveyed the scene outside. The surfers had obviously been out for hours and she watched for a moment as one, more intrepid than the rest, rode a wave all the way into the beach.

What energy, she thought. She could use some of it herself. She would have to get to the supermarket as soon as she'd managed to throw on a few clothes and grabbed something to eat.

In the kitchen she plugged in the kettle, still dwelling on thoughts of the barbecue meeting on the beach last night. The enthusiasm of Jamie and his friends had been infectious and she had felt herself caught up in their plans and dreams. Coasteering was a completely new concept to her, and yet she could see how it could catch on. She had a sudden vision of inaccessible cliffs populated with figures having the time of their lives, seabirds screeching and whirling overhead. The wonder of it was that Rob hadn't mentioned coasteering, but perhaps they hadn't started it up in New Zealand yet.

Rob, she thought now, as she took a carton of orange juice out of the fridge. In the firelight that blazed into the starry sky last night she had seen Jamie's pleased expression change quickly to one of dismay when she had made it clear that the last thing she wanted was to have Rob show up here.

She slumped down at the table, and sat with her head in her hands. Jamie seemed to think that Rob was reconsidering his plans to return to New Zealand and she had to admit that he could be right. Not much had been said after that, but she could see that Jamie was thinking things through. Rob was exactly what they were looking for at *Leapaway* and was it fair to Jamie to try and stop him coming down here?

She was still worrying about it when she was

at the supermarket, avoiding the queue at Zena's checkout and hoping she didn't spot her as she grabbed the milk and ran. Zena would be involved in this decision, too, because Jamie would be sure to tell her. And what might she think of all this?

Carina found out sooner than she expected, because Zena phoned her at lunchtime suggesting a meeting after work that day. 'How about a coffee at the beach café, the small place on the other side of the beach from you with a fantastic view?'

'Sounds good,' said Carina. 'I'll be there, Zena. What time?'

'Seven? You'll have seen the new people in by then. I've got things to do afterwards but I need to fill you in on a thing or two first. See you!'

Carina arrived at the café in plenty of time and found Zena already there, seated at a table on the balcony, a mug of coffee in front of her. She sprang up on seeing Carina. 'Coffee?'

'I'll get it,' said Carina.

She was back within minutes.

'Jamie wants me to have a word with you,' Zena said.

'I see,' said Carina. 'Or rather, I don't.'

Zena leaned forward. '*Leapaway*'s a new thing,' she said. 'We need to get it off the ground fast. And now we've got a small group interested and they want to start tomorrow. It'll be good for business, you see. It's important.'

Carina nodded. 'I can see that. But where do I come in?'

'There are four of them between the ages of ten and fifteen and a couple of adults. Trouble is, they need last-minute accommodation, and Jamie thought of you?'

'Me?'

Zena looked at Carina, her dark eyes full of hope. 'Your properties. He thinks it would solve two problems in one. Our clients will have somewhere to stay, and another of your apartments is let for the week. They'd pay the seven day tariff, of course.'

'He wants me to check with Belinda?'

'Could you do that?'

'She's away for a couple of days.'

'Her mobile?'

'Well, yes, okay, I'll try when I get back to Spray Point. Will that do? I didn't bring my phone with me.'

Zena smiled. 'You'll let me know at once, won't you? I'll write my number down for you. Oh, and we want to know a bit more about that chap who's applied for a job with *Leapaway,* the one you know who sounds so perfect?'

'Rob can't be serious wanting to work down here,' Carina said. 'He's already got a job.'

'Not according to Jamie. And we need someone with his qualifications.' She finished her coffee and got to her feet. 'I must get back.'

Carina drank her coffee and stood up, too. She followed Zena up the steps to the cliff path.

'You'll go back now and phone Belinda?' Zena said. 'Those people will be turning up early tomorrow and I'll need to tell them something then.'

Carina watched Zena go, deep in thought. Belinda would surely be pleased to get extra custom for her properties and Jamie's idea of putting bookings her way could only be a good thing. Couldn't it?

Belinda wasn't answering her mobile. Carina left a message on voice mail hoping she would get back to her. When she didn't, she decided to make the decision herself and phoned Zena to say that 22 Pengellert Apartments would be ready for occupation from ten o'clock the following morning.

She knew that all was in order there, apart from the orange juice and milk that Belinda liked to provide, but they would be easy enough to pick up on the way over there next day.

So at nine thirty next morning, pleased that

everything was ready, Carina slid open the patio door to sit on the balcony and wait at the apartment. Her mobile rang. Startled, she saw the caller was Belinda.

'I need you over at Pengellert Apartments right away. You'll have got 22 ready for occupancy, I hope?'

'That's where I am, Belinda. I tried to phone you . . .'

'Some people are arriving almost at once to view the place. I'll see you over there, Carina, in a few moments.'

Horrified, Carina sprang up. Now what was she going to do?

*   *   *

'Indeed, I'm hoping she'll come again,' said Taryn Curnow, moving a little in his armchair to get more comfortable.

'Here, let me,' Mrs Trent said, rushing forward to give him some assistance.

He shrugged her away, blinking a little in the strong sunlight slanting in through the window of the nursing home. 'Relax, Sarah, my dear. Sit down over there and let me look at you. That's better. There's no need to worry about me, I assure you I may be an old man but I've still got my faculties. Why shouldn't I see this girl if she's happy to come?'

Sarah Trent sighed, remembering the harsh comments that Marcus had come out with

92

when he realised who Carina was. 'Marcus doesn't really know her, you see.'

'It's nothing to do with knowing her, my dear. Marcus would object to anyone getting in on the act.'

'Getting in on the act? Whatever can you mean?'

'Don't play the innocent with me, Sarah. We all know how Marcus operates. Always had an eye on the main chance since he was a nipper. He won't want competition now.'

Sarah's cheeks felt warm and her chair creaked as she fidgeted.

'Marcus has got a head on his shoulders, I'll give him that,' Taryn went on. 'He was a grand boy before he got ideas into that head of his. And he hasn't been to see me for months.'

'He's so busy now,' Sarah Trent said. 'Did I tell you about this new business venture Jamie's starting? Marcus has some idea about investing in it. I'm not sure it's a good thing.'

'I heard something or other but I couldn't make head nor tail of it. "Coasteering"? Never heard of it.'

Sarah leaned forward, anxious to tell him all she knew about something she wasn't at all sure about. It all sounded so casual.

'But don't you need capital to set up something like that?' Taryn said, when she had finished.

'I suppose so,' she said doubtfully.

'Well, what d'you know? That young

stepson of yours coming up with an idea like that reminds me of when I started out thinking the world was my oyster . . .' He broke off, coughing.

Sarah looked at Taryn anxiously and then poured water from the jug and handed the glass to him, supporting it for him.

'Don't fuss so, Sarah. I can cope. There's plenty of life in me yet.'

'I certainly hope so,' she said.

He looked at her shrewdly. 'Really?'

'Yes, really,' Sarah insisted.

'Why doesn't Marcus come to see me any more? You can tell him from me that when I'm gone, things might turn out differently than he expects. Oh yes. Just you wait and see!'

The doorbell of the apartment rang, making Carina jump. Leaping up from her chair on the balcony, she went through the sitting-room to the hall and pressed the intercom button. 'Hello? We got here!' The excitement in the young voice almost made her take a step back. 'I'll be right down,' she said.

The six of them were waiting for her outside, clutching bags and buoyancy aids. 'We've brought our own, you see,' one of the young boys said proudly.

'Mr and Mrs Dawkins?' Carina said. 'Come on up.'

There was nothing else to do but show them the accommodation, hoping that by some miracle Belinda wouldn't arrive with the people she had booked in. A traffic jam somewhere holding things up for days, a fallen tree blocking their route, a flood . . .

'Wonderful,' said Mrs Dawkins. 'We're going to like it here, aren't we, folks? You girls had better have the twin room and the boys can kip down in here.'

Carina demonstrated how the sofa turned into a bed at the press of a button. Then the family all crowded around to look at the view from the balcony, exclaiming loudly about what they were going to do as soon as they were settled into this fabulous place.

Down below, looking up in disbelief, was Belinda. With her were two people.

'Excuse me for a moment,' Carina said. Downstairs she emerged into the breezy air; the enormity of what she had done hitting her like a tidal wave. Two people expected to move into the luxury accommodation she had just given to someone else. A sacking offence, this, without a doubt. When her mobile rang, she pulled it out of her pocket with shaking fingers.

'What's going on?' Belinda's voice barked.

'A misunderstanding . . .'

'On whose part?'

'I need to speak to you about this.'

'Get back to Spray Point at once and wait there,' Belinda ordered. Carina did so, her legs feeling weak as she parked the van and got out.

A car jolted up the rutted road and turned into the entrance. Her mouth dry, she moved forward to greet Belinda, an apology on her lips.

'Save your breath,' Belinda ordered. 'The damage has been done. Did it not occur to you that taking so much responsibility on yourself was not the wisest thing to do? I need reliability for this job.'

Carina quailed.

'I had to contact one of our rivals, who luckily had a vacancy. Very much against the grain, especially as these people are looking for a place to book for next year, too. That's income for us well and truly lost. They won't come back to us.'

'I tried to contact you,' Carina said. 'When I couldn't get hold of you, I thought I'd better use my own initiative.'

'I'm tempted to terminate our business arrangement and send you packing.'

Carina swallowed hard. 'That isn't fair.'

'Fair? Who said anything about fair? I know nothing about these people and neither do you. Are they creditworthy? Do you even know that?'

Carina was silent. She had done her best to apologise for doing something she had thought might be helpful. She could do no more.

AN EXHILARATING EXPERIENCE

Tullick Head jutted out into the calm sea, low rocky cliffs providing no easy way up from the water that looked translucent as it rippled among the rocks. A truly peaceful scene, Carina thought, as she stood on the edge of the cliffs this bright morning. Jamie had chosen an easy route for *Leapaway*'s first clients, the small group of four children looking absurdly young in their wetsuits and helmets.

She had felt a strong compulsion to monitor the Dawley family on their first coasteering outing. Jamie had been delighted with her decision, pressing her to stay with them all day. But of course, that wasn't possible.

She looked round now for the Dawley children's parents, but couldn't see them.

'The kids are on their own this morning,' said Jamie, appearing beside her. He was dressed in his wetsuit and his fair hair was ruffled. 'Mum and Dad Dawley opted to stay behind. There wasn't room for them all in my van anyway, with all the equipment.'

'This is it, then,' Carina said. 'Your first

session. I hope it all goes well.'

He nodded. 'Thanks for coming.'

'But what use will I be up here just watching?'

'You've got your mobile?'

'My mobile?' She didn't like the sound of that. Surely it wasn't so dangerous that she'd be needed to call the emergency services? How would any heavy vehicle get here, anyway? There was barely enough room to park their two vehicles. They'd have to do a helicopter rescue. Belinda would have a field day with that if the local Press got hold of the story and reported exactly where the children were staying to enable them to take part in *Leapaway*'s activities. She doubted that she would consider any publicity as good publicity.

'Just in case,' Jamie said, smiling. 'No worries, really.'

'I hope not.'

'Trust me.'

She smiled back at him. His confidence was infectious.

'Zena was supposed to come but opted out at the last moment,' Jamie said, as he put his helmet on. 'There's someone else who was supposed to be here, a qualified firstaider name of Barry Jenks, but he hasn't shown either.'

'Will you be all right on your own?'

'Have to be.'

'But is that allowed, only one leader?'

He shrugged. 'There are only four of them. And they're kids.'

'All the same . . .'

'Want to come with us?'

Carina hesitated. 'What would I have to do?'

'Follow on behind to count heads, that's all. I plan to do a low jump-off over there on that flat piece of jutting-out rock and then a swim round to a place further along where we can scramble up the cliff. It's a good route for beginners.'

Carina looked to where Jamie indicated. It didn't seem very far to reach by swimming. 'Okay, then,' she said.

'You can use Zena's wetsuit. And we've plenty of helmets. Change in the van, why don't you? It's a changing room, office, you name it.' He grinned. 'But not for much longer, once the cash starts rolling in.'

Carina smiled. He sounded so proud that she couldn't help but be pleased for him.

'Don't forget to grab a buoyancy aid,' he shouted after her.

Pulling on the wetsuit took several minutes longer than she expected and so did lacing up the buoyancy aid. Then she selected a helmet and joined the others outside where Jamie was explaining what was going to happen.

'We're part of a team,' he was saying. 'You're responsible all the time for the person in front of you, so make sure they're all right.

That's the rule. Understood?'

The four children nodded, looking solemn.

'Okay then, let's go.'

Carina had thought that the jump was only a small one, but the rock seemed much higher when it came to her turn. The others were bobbing about in the water in their orange buoyancy aids, shouting encouragement. She closed her eyes, jumped, and was soon bobbing about, too. A pleasant sensation. She glanced up at the cliff and saw masses of sea pinks growing in clefts near the top, looking pretty against the dark background. She swam behind the others to the place where the scramble back up the cliff was possible.

After much splashing and shrieks of enjoyment, the four youngsters were soon out of the water and scrambling up the low rocky cliff after Jamie. Reaching the top, they shouted for Carina to join them.

She felt surprisingly elated as she stood beside them, breathing heavily.

'Okay everyone?' said Jamie.

'Brilliant!'

'Great!'

'Can we do it again?'

'Please!'

Carina was as eager as the others to do the same thing again, but this time Jamie took them further along the cliff path to where they had to do some manoeuvring across rocks and along a narrow ledge.

'That's enough,' Jamie said at last, ignoring their cries of protest. 'Lunch now and then back to Mum and Dad to see if they want to join in the afternoon session.'

Carina felt tired but exhilarated at the same time. 'I can't believe I've just done that,' she marvelled. The experience had been so fantastic she had no idea how long they had taken. It must be the most easily accessible, ultimate get-away-from-your-worries activity, because, within reason, anyone could do it.

She and the two girls changed out of their wetsuits in the van and emerged laughing and talking. The boys were on a high, too, demanding even greater cliff routes for the afternoon session.

Carina glanced at her watch. 'I must get back,' she said.

'What's the rush?' Jamie said. 'You saw the lunch hampers in the van. Plenty for all.'

'Not for me.'

'Lighten up, Carina. You're creating the wrong atmosphere. These people are on holiday, remember.'

'But I'm not,' she reminded him. 'And I'm already in trouble because of arranging accommodation for them. I don't want to make things worse by being away for too long.'

'Belinda should be down on her knees to you in gratitude for getting another property booked up for the week,' Jamie said.

'She likes to vet her clients herself,' Carina explained.

'Well, the Dawleys are obviously not from outer space, so what's the worry?'

'It makes good sense,' said Carina shortly.

'Then go, if that's the way you feel.'

The words, *And don't come back*, seemed to hover in the air.

*   *   *

Carina's orders for the afternoon were to remain at Spray Point to take delivery of three small TV sets. The message from Belinda was on the answer phone when she got back and she was to acknowledge the call as soon as she received it.

'Where were you?' asked Belinda, when she did so. 'I phoned half an hour ago.'

'Just checking that all was well with the Dawleys,' Carina said. 'The children had their first coasteering session.'

'I trust they didn't drown themselves.'

*   *   *

Carina prepared a sandwich lunch and carried it out of doors to enjoy on the grassy bank behind the bungalow. The sunshine was warm, and tired from her exertions this morning, she was glad to lie back with her eyes closed and listen to the soothing sound of the sea.

She hadn't meant to sleep. The sound of a delivery van reversing its way out of the drive woke her. She leapt up, heart thudding, in time to see the vehicle disappearing into the distance.

Hastily she gathered up her plate. To find the three boxes containing the television sets on the front doorstep was unlikely, but she couldn't help hoping that by some chance they would be there. Fool. Why should they be left there in the open for all the world to see when her signature was required?

*   *   *

Annabel phoned later in the afternoon. 'How goes it then, Carina?'

'Not too badly,' Carina replied. Hearing her friend's voice was wonderful and she felt immediately cheered. Belinda had not yet got back to her about the non-delivery of the TV sets, but it could only be a matter of time.

'Have you been to see the old man again? I thought you said he was pleased to see you?'

'My great-uncle,' said Carina. Even now she could hardly believe it. He was such a nice old man that she felt sorry she couldn't be there for him every day 'I'm hoping to go again on Wednesday,' she said. 'So, how are things with you?'

'Bad. Very bad. Can't stand it at work any

103

longer, so I've taken some leave. Two weeks starting on Friday. So, how about you? Are you being overworked by that slave driver?'

'Well, I've a meeting to go to tomorrow afternoon, a trustee meeting for the apartments. I'm supposed to be representing Belinda and I'll have to take notes and report back. And I think there's one for the cottages on Thursday.'

'Makes a change from cleaning up after people.'

'I'll be doing that on Friday. I've another lot coming into the cottage as well as to the apartments.'

'Have the other cleaners turned up yet?'

'I need to wait and see what's what,' Carina said evasively. Then she broke down.

'Annabel, I may be in serious trouble.'

To see Jamie coming up the path to Spray Point that evening wasn't as much a surprise to Carina as he obviously thought it would be.

'I was out of order this morning,' he said, as she went to meet him. 'I'm really sorry, Carina.'

'How did it go this afternoon?'

'You're not mad at me?'

She smiled. 'I can recognise stress when I see it.'

'You're a girl in a million.'

104

'Belinda doesn't think so.'

'Pack the job in then, and come and work for me.'

Surprised, she stared at him. 'At *Leapaway?*'

'A chap called Tony who's applied to join us showed up this afternoon for a try-out. Afraid of heights, would you believe? No good to us.'

'Poor Tony.'

'Poor us, you mean. Zena mucked in this afternoon and helped out. Those Dawley kids are really keen. I nearly gave you a buzz.'

'It wouldn't have done any good, Jamie. I had to be on duty here' Not that she had been much use, asleep at her post, she thought. 'Coming in?'

'Why not?' he said. 'I've something else to ask you.'

The phone rang as they stepped into the hall.

'Carina?' Belinda barked. 'The TVs were delivered here instead of Spray Point. I need them moved immediately. Bring the van round at once.'

'Does she have to bellow like that?' Jamie said. 'I heard every word.'

'Then you'll know she needs me at her house.'

'I need you.'

'But she needs me more.'

'I doubt that,' Jamie said, stepping forward and taking Carina in his arms.

His kiss was warm and gentle and for a

second she relaxed against him. Then she struggled free. 'Jamie, please! I'm in real trouble here.'

He caught hold of both her shoulders. 'Anything I can help with?'

She breathed deeply. 'I'll get the sack'

'As bad as that? Come on, Carina, I need to hear more about this.'

Confiding in Jamie was so easy. When she had finished, he said, 'You have several options. She won't give you the push. You're too valuable to her for that. I saw this place when Zena worked for her and I can tell you there's a vast difference now. Talk about efficiency, you've got it in bucketloads and it's just what we need at *Leapaway*.'

Carina frowned. Who wanted to be described as efficient? Certainly not her. Beautiful, charming, intelligent, yes. But not efficient. It seemed more like an insult than a compliment.

'Seriously, Carina, why not give my offer some thought?'

'And where would I live?'

'Zena might have some ideas. So if Belinda lays in to you when you see her, you'll have no hesitation, will you, in giving *her* the push?'

Carina smiled. 'I'd better get round there now.'

'I'll come with you and give you a hand with the TVs. Then I'm taking you to the *Surge And Swell*. My way of thinking you for this morning.'

'Not to mention a bit of bribery to join *Leapaway*,' Carina grinned.

In the event, the following evening was more convenient for Jamie to take her to the *Surge And Swell* because something had cropped up that needed his personal attention, he said. Carina was happy to postpone their meeting and they arranged to meet at eight o'clock.

The *Surge And Swell* surprised her. With a name like that and so near the busy end of the beach, she had expected a sea and surfing theme. Instead, a stylish interior greeted her. The pale green walls were bare of ornament and the marble-topped tables each had a vase of fresh white roses. Soft music played and the other diners' voices were a pleasant murmur.

Jamie had already arrived and was seated at a table in the corner. 'No view from here, I'm afraid,' he said, getting up to greet her. She smiled and sat down. 'Never mind. It's lovely in here' She had changed into a flowery skirt and plain white blouse and Jamie was wearing an open-neck shirt and new jeans.

He handed her the menu. 'The salmon tranche with fresh lime and ginger sauce is their speciality. I can recommend it.'

She was happy to make the choice. Jamie consulted the wine list and selected a bottle of

Semillon Chardonnay.

'So how did today's *Leapaway* session go?' Carina asked.

He frowned. 'There wasn't one. I'm not too sure of this Tim Denton I went to see, so I decided to wait till Zena's free again tomorrow and another chap I know is back. The Dawleys have booked in again, all six of them this time.'

'That's good.'

'We'll do Tullick Head again. After that, if they're up to it, I might move on further up the coast and do some scrambling round the caves you can't reach by boat, or any other way apart from the route we'll take.'

Carina took a sip of the ice-cold wine. 'That sounds difficult.'

'We'll see.'

'You'll be careful?'

His eyes were alight with amusement. 'I'm fully qualified, I'll have you know, and so are the others.'

'Zena?'

'Zena's quite a girl. There'll be three of us, at least, but it would be better still if you were with us.'

He leaned forward. 'Have you thought any more about joining us, Carina?'

'Don't I need qualifications?' she said doubtfully.

He brushed this aside with easy confidence. 'You can get those fairly easily if you're keen.'

'I don't want to let Belinda down, but the

new cleaners she's promised haven't turned up yet.'

'Seems to me she's no intention of getting you any more help.'

'She's busy,' Carina said. 'Her husband's in hospital, don't forget. She's a lot to think about.'

'All the more reason for getting the cleaning side of things properly organised. You can't be expected to do it all yourself.'

'No, I know that.'

Carina had thought this herself more than once, but she couldn't believe Belinda would deliberately keep her short-staffed.

Afterwards, they walked hand in hand across the beach to Spray Point. The setting sun cast streaks of light on the sea, and the clouds on the horizon were deep orange.

As they reached the beginning of the steps, Jamie stopped and kissed her, his lips gentle and tasting faintly of peach from the wine. It was a magic moment she wished could go on forever.

He released her as someone came up behind them, wanting to pass. Jamie moved over. 'Sorry,' he said. Then, 'Ah, Tim. I didn't see you there.'

'Otherwise engaged? Well, I don't blame you.' The tall, thin young man stood regarding them. 'I've been looking for you, Jamie. The girl I saw at the *Leapaway* van said I'd find you at the *Surge And Swell*.' He sounded accusing.

'That's where we were,' said Jamie. 'So what do you want?'

'Can we walk and talk at the same time?'

'Lead the way.'

They followed him up the steps. At the top, Tim seemed in no hurry to divulge his reason for contacting Jamie but talked of other coasteering firms and what their aims were as they started to walk together across the grass to the road.

'So what exactly are you getting at?' Jamie said.

'Coasteering is the ultimate adrenaline high,' Tim said.

'I can't quarrel with that.'

'Nor me. It tests the limits of all who take part. I like that.'

'Who wouldn't?'

They were walking up the road to Spray Point now. Jamie squeezed Carina's hand as they reached the entrance to the bungalow and stopped. She shivered.

'Cold?' said Jamie in concern.

'A bit.'

'Then go on up and I'll see you tomorrow.'

'Thanks for a lovely meal,' she said, feeling her words inadequate. 'Thanks for your company.'

Maybe it was just as well the evening should end here, she thought, as she ran lightly up the steps to Spray Point. She had enough to do coping with Belinda's demands, without any added emotional complications.

A VISITOR SHOCKS CARINA

The elderly lady Carina had seen on her first visit to Madrenna Nursing Home was the sole occupant of the sunny sitting room on the ground floor when she called in on Wednesday afternoon.

'Ah, there you are, my dear,' the old lady said, her smile lighting up her pleasant face. 'Your great-uncle won't be long. Come and sit down near me. Carina, isn't it? Such a pretty name.'

'He told you who I am?' Carina said, as she seated herself in the chintz-covered armchair, the present she had brought with her on her lap.

'Indeed he did, my dear. He was so pleased you took the trouble to visit him. He's so fond of you.'

Carina smiled. 'And I'm fond of him. He's such a nice man.'

'Oh he is. The vicar's here, you know. That's where Taryn is, talking to him in the office. I'm sure he won't be long.' She smiled. 'But I haven't introduced myself. I'm Rosa Marshall, a widow now for many years.'

'And have you lived here long, Mrs Marshall?'

111

'Rosa, please,' Mrs Marshall said, and went on, 'I could no longer manage on my own, I had a charming house on the edge of town, but it was far too large for one person. At this time of year the roses are a picture, deep pink against the white of the walls . . . ' She broke off and looked wistful for a moment.

Carina could easily imagine her sadness at having to leave her home. The marvel was that the older woman didn't appear despondent about her situation. In fact, she gave off a glow of contentment.

'Your garden sounds beautiful,' Carina said.

'Oh, it was, my dear, but it was hard to find gardeners, and of course, I couldn't do much after my husband died. Such a relief not to have to worry about that now and to be looked after so well.'

'Yes, I suppose so.'

'And the family approved. My eldest is in the States, you know, and the girls are away studying hotel management. I came here just before your great-uncle moved in.' She looked up. 'Ah, here he is now.'

Today, Taryn's scarf was striped in blues and yellows. Carina smiled to see his eager gait, although the matron held on to him, urging caution. She settled him in his chair with his walking stick at his side and left.

'This is for me?' he said, when Carina handed him the box of chocolates she had brought. 'How kind you are, my dear. And I

112

see you and Rosa have already met.'

The visit was pleasant and they talked of quiet, comfortable things. Taryn reminisced about his boyhood at Poltizzy and Carina listened eagerly.

When at last she got up to go they both pressed her to come again.

'As soon as I get another free afternoon,' she promised.

*   *   *

Afterwards, Carina ignored the turning to Spray Point and drove straight on to the car park for Poltyre Head. An impulsive decision but a good one, she thought, as she got out of the car to walk to the tip of the headland. She needed a breath of air after the cosy atmosphere of the nursing home, where she had left her great-uncle and Rosa enjoying afternoon tea together. And there was plenty of air up here. On either side the sea heaved and swelled as it built up to reach the shore in huge surfable waves.

Her head was buzzing with what she had just been hearing. Her family history! It had all happened a long time ago, but she felt so much closer to her father now. And certainly more so than when he had been alive, away from home a lot trying to cope with the loss of his young wife, the mother she had never known.

113

Following a wide path, Carina made for the end of the point for the best view on either side. She would explore some of the other paths that led nearer to the cliff edge another time.

She felt in her pocket for her mobile phone, fingering it but leaving it there. Sadie was at work at the moment and wouldn't be able to talk. This evening then. Being able to confide her delight about her great-uncle in someone who had her interests at heart was something to look forward to. And then she would hear about the preparations Sadie was making for her birdwatching holiday in Devon.

The invigorating breeze was stronger today, and the flowery turf beneath Carina's feet was springy. She caught the scent of wild thyme as she walked, then she sat down on the seat at the end of the path.

The cliffs here were more dramatic than at Tullick Head and jagged rocks loomed out of the water, looking distinctly dangerous with the surging water hurling itself against them in bursts of spray. Jamie wouldn't find it easy to manoeuvre his way round these. There could well be caves, though. He had told her that one of the aims of coasteering was to explore inaccessible places.

What a super way to earn a living. She envied him, doing something that gave him the chance to provide something of great value and satisfaction to others.

She was glad she had come all the way to the tip of the headland. The last few days had been difficult, as Belinda had taken over three more holiday cottages at Loveday Place and expected Carina to cope with the cleaning and decorating of those, too. And after the fiasco with the non-delivery of the TV sets, she felt in no position to refuse.

This was especially so when she and Jamie had arrived on Belinda's doorstep to collect the sets and had learned that her husband, in hospital for the last week, had to have an emergency operation.

So, not a good moment to enquire about more cleaning help and to ask why none had yet been forthcoming. This was going to be a major problem, now Carina wanted more free time to visit Taryn.

Back at Spray Point, she changed into her work clothes, but before she set off for Loveday Place, she switched the computer on to check her emails. Three new ones . . . bookings. Belinda would be pleased.

She checked the chart for June. Yes, the vacancies were there.

She loved replying to emails like these, confirming the dates and requesting deposits. The replies from the clients always sounded so happy and excited.

A job well done.

The ringing of the door bell as Carina was finishing breakfast next morning surprised her. The postman with a parcel for her? Unlikely, but she wasn't expecting anyone else.

Through the frosted glass of the front door she saw the shape of a dark figure. The door was sticking as usual and needed a strong yank to pull it open. Outside, his face stiff with disapproval, was Marcus Trent.

'Miss Curnow?'

Surely he couldn't have forgotten already that they had already met. 'That's me,' she said.

'I've come to speak with you.'

'I'm afraid it hasn't yet been delivered.'

For a moment he looked disconcerted. 'What hasn't?'

'The solicitor's letter you kindly told me to expect.'

'Can we go inside?'

'That's not possible. Anything you have to say can be said here.' She had a sudden alarming thought. 'It's not bad news is it? My great-uncle . . . ?'

His face darkened. '*Your* great-uncle?'

'Taryn Curnow of Poltizzy House, my grandfather's brother,' she said proudly. No way was she going to be intimidated by this man.

'I understand you've been bothering him

116

again. This has got to stop. I must insist.'

'And why is that?'

'My family have been looking after the old man's welfare for many years. We have his interests at heart. When I learnt that you were coming to work here and that your name was Curnow, I knew you would be trouble. And I wasn't wrong. You didn't waste any time finding the Nursing Home, did you? Just as well I was there to warn you off.'

'Have the Madrenna people instructed you to warn me off?'

She saw a flash of anger in his dark eyes. 'What right have you to come now, at this late stage, claiming relationship, worming your way into his confidence?'

'I don't think that's any business of yours.'

'Indeed it is. Your insinuating yourself into his life appears to have had the effect you wanted. My mother is most upset.'

'What do you mean, Mr Trent?'

His smouldering dark looks seemed menacing now and Carina took a step back.

'We've been deeply shocked to hear his ramblings about the need to change his will.'

Carina looked at Marcus Trent in dismay. 'But . . .'

'Do you deny it?'

'Deny that he's changing his will? How would I know that? It's got nothing to do with me.'

'Do you deny that you've been visiting him

117

with a view to getting him to change his will?'

'Of course I deny it!' Carina replied hotly. 'I like visiting Taryn, that's all.'

'I suggest that in future you leave him alone, or it will be the worse for you.' And with that, Marcus Trent turned on his heels and left.

Dumbfounded, Carina watched him march down the steps to where he had left his car. Moments later he drove off.

She closed the door and locked it and for several shocked moments stood leaning against it. She couldn't begin to understand what all that was about. On the surface, of course, it was easy. Marcus Trent believed she had shown up here to be on hand to claim part of an inheritance. But there was something beneath the surface here that she couldn't quite fathom.

Thoughtfully, Carina returned to the kitchen. She couldn't tell any of this to Sadie, of course, or she would worry. Phoning home yesterday evening, hoping for a long chat, she had been disappointed that Sadie hadn't been there. Instead, Rob had answered the phone, sounding distant and uninterested. The conversation had been stilted, which didn't surprise her, because he was the last person who would understand her pleasure in finding a relative of her own.

'You're okay, Carina, aren't you?' Rob said, just before she rang off.

'Very much so,' she said, wondering at his

sudden concern.

And she had been all right then. But not now. Now she wished there was someone she could talk to about Marcus' unprovoked attack on her integrity. Zena would listen, she thought, as she contemplated her interrupted breakfast. But Zena was a friend of Jamie's and had once been keen on Marcus. A Trent family friend, you could say.

Annabel, of course!

'I'm coming down this evening,' her friend said, when she heard what Carina had to tell her. 'No, don't argue. I'll come complete with sleeping bag and a coolbox full of goodies. I've got two weeks off, and what better way to spend them than by helping you out.'

'Oh Annabel, that's great. Are you sure . . .'

'I'll give you a buzz when I get near and you can tell me where to find you. See you soon, and don't worry!'

Carina smiled as she tipped away her uneaten bran flakes and cleared the table. Annabel was amazing. She had this wonderful way of making people feel uplifted. She was a good friend and would understand the position at once and back Carina without question in whatever she decided to do.

Why should she let Marcus Trent dictate to her? She had done nothing wrong and she had no ulterior motives. That anyone should suspect her of trying to worm her way into Taryn's affections for financial reasons was

119

deeply hurtful. She thought of his kind face and his delight in her company. Was she to deprive him of that, on Marcus Trent's say-so?

ANNABEL HAS SOME NEWS

Annabel smoothed her skirt over her knees and cleared her throat. 'There's something you need to know, Carina. You won't be mad at me or anything for not coming out with it before?'

'Sounds intriguing,' said Carina, leaning back in her chair and regarding her friend affectionately.

They were seated on garden chairs on the patio at the front of Spray Point, having enjoyed an al fresco meal supplied by Annabel. Eating out here had been her idea, late as it was, because the evening was so lovely and she wanted to hear the cries of homing seagulls and the swishing surge of the sea down below against the rocks.

'You won't think it's intriguing when you hear what it is,' said Annabel.

Carina put down her empty glass on the low table between them. 'Out with it, then.'

'I waited till now on purpose,' Annabel said. 'I thought we'd eat first and get all the talk of Marcus out of the way. I can't believe he threatened you like that.'

Carina shuddered. 'Neither can I.'

'You're not still worried about him?'

'I'm not going to let him get to me, if that's what you mean. So, what have you got to tell me?'

'You're not going to like it.'

'Annabel, get on with it.'

'I saw Rob at the hospital when I was leaving work. He was in the waiting room looking as white as that seagull up there. He didn't want me to say anything, but he didn't swear me to secrecy, either.'

Carina was concerned. 'What was wrong with him?' she asked anxiously.

'Not Rob. Sadie. She . . . well, she had a bit of a fall.'

Carina shot upright in her seat. 'A fall? When? Is she badly hurt?'

'She's okay apart from a broken wrist. She thought you'd worry if you knew about it.'

'Worry? Of course I'm worried. But how . . .?'

'Getting her suitcase down from the attic.'

'When was this?'

'Yesterday. She was at the hospital and they kept her in overnight. She'll be home by now. She's all right, Carina, honestly.'

'I rang home last evening,' said Carina. 'Rob should have told me. That's him all over, thinking he's the only one who cares.'

'Oh come on, Carina, be fair. He was only obeying his mum's orders.'

Carina stared down at her empty plate. She

121

could imagine Sadie being adamant that he was to say nothing. 'But how will Sadie manage? I'll have to go home,' she said.

'Rob's there. I don't suppose he's completely useless.'

'I suppose so. All the same, I should be there.'

'And what could you do that Rob can't?'

Annabel offered Carina the last biscuit and then took it herself when she waved the packet away.

Carina had been ravenous when they had carried the chairs and table outside. The smoked salmon and brie-filled baguettes Annabel had provided were mouth-watering and so were the luscious cream-filled chocolate éclairs. Now, she couldn't eat anything.

'I couldn't do much, I suppose,' she admitted. 'But it's Sadie's bird-watching holiday coming up. She's booked into a self-catering place in a village near Exmouth. Woodbury, I think.'

'Yes, I see. That accounts for the suitcase.'

'Oh, poor Sadie. She was so looking forward to it. I'll give her a phone now.'

'You'll land me in it if you do,' Annabel said.

'You don't think that's going to stop me?'

Her friend laughed. 'I wouldn't think much of you if it did.'

To Carina's surprise, Sadie sounded cheerful when she spoke to her while Annabel was making coffee. 'My right wrist, would you believe?' she said. 'How stupid is that?'

'I wish I could pack it in here and come and look after you.'

'Nonsense, love. I'm perfectly all right. And Rob's here, remember.'

Yes, Rob was there and would be a help to his mother. No way could he leave her and come down here now, coasteering or no coasteering.

'And you're sure you can manage?' Carina asked anxiously.

'It was a bit of a shock at first, that's all. Anyway, what would your Belinda do without you?'

'You've got a point there.'

Carina glanced at Annabel through the front window. She was placing the mugs of coffee on the table ready for when the phone call was finished. How glad she was that her friend had alerted her to Sadie's problems, even though she couldn't do much for her from here.

'You know Annabel's here with me?' she said.

'She is?'

'She's going to help me with the cleaning and everything. Isn't that great? I hope

Belinda's pleased. Annabel's only here for two weeks, of course, but she'll be such a help.'

'So she'll stay with you at Spray Point?'

'Tonight, anyway. I'll have to clear it with Belinda tomorrow.'

They talked a little longer and then rang off. Carina paused for a moment with her hand on the phone. Should she contact Belinda tonight? No, too late now. There was room for Annabel at Spray Point, and surely there would be no problem with that?

At first Belinda sounded suspicious when she was contacted the following morning, and Carina was afraid her reaction would be the same as it had been for the Dawley family and their friends.

'I'll come round at once,' she said.

'Oh dear,' Carina said as she put the phone down. 'Prepare yourself for a visitation from the boss, Annabel.'

'All systems go,' Annabel said. 'I'd better do my face and comb my hair.'

Carina laughed. Annabel's curly hair always looked immaculate and there was no problem at all with her face, except sometimes when she delighted in pulling her mouth into funny shapes to make people laugh. Hopefully, she wouldn't be doing that this morning.

The breakfast washing-up was done and the

kitchen tidied before Belinda parked her car alongside the van down below and began the climb up to the front door. She was wearing her baggy trousers again, topped with a man's striped jacket over her broad figure.

'We've left the chairs and table outside from last night,' said Annabel, when she spied Belinda. 'A hanging offence, at least.'

'Shut up,' Carina said, and went to open the door.

'I've advertised for more help,' Belinda said, in reply to Carina's greeting. 'You'd think there would be someone out there glad of a job for the summer, but the only applicants were highly unsuitable.'

'So I'm in with a chance then?' said Annabel, appearing behind Carina.

'This is Annabel,' Carina said.

'Hmm,' was all Belinda said.

Carina hesitated, not knowing whether that response indicated approval. 'We've got the kettle on for coffee, Belinda,' she said.

'I've no time for that,' said Belinda. 'I'm due at the hospital in an hour.'

Carina was immediately concerned, noting the pallor of the older woman's face and the lines deeply etched round her mouth. 'How is your husband?'

Belinda frowned. 'So-so.'

Carina hesitated. Belinda didn't sound as if she would welcome further interest.

'So would you like me to help out here temporarily?' Annabel said, in the tone of one conferring a great favour.

'There's another booking,' Belinda said to Carina, ignoring Annabel. 'You can put them into Thrift Cottage when the present occupants leave on Sunday. They phoned late last night. Make a note of that, will you?'

'I'll do it straight away.'

Annabel moved forward. 'I'm here to help, if you'll have me.' Belinda looked her up and down critically. 'Well, I suppose you're better than nothing.'

'Definitely better than nothing. You won't find anyone better.'

'That's as may be.'

'So am I in or not?'

'I need Annabel here, since she's good enough to offer,' Carina said to Belinda. 'She'll be invaluable to me with all the cleaning we've got to do.'

Belinda gave a half-smile. 'Very well. The minimum rate of pay, and don't expect more.'

'The cheek of it,' Annabel said, when Belinda had gone. 'If it wasn't for you, Carina, I'd tell her where to put her mouldy old job. Anyone can see she's desperate for help. Why doesn't she admit it? I don't know about you, but I'm having a coffee now, this instant, like it or not.'

'Calm down,' said Carina, smiling. 'I'm having one too. I'm your immediate boss, remember, and that's an order.'

Annabel laughed, her annoyance immediately forgotten.

On Carina's next visit to Madrenna Nursing Home, Annabel came with her. 'I want to see this wonderful relative of yours,' she said. 'And I'll act as your bodyguard if the malevolent Marcus shows up. I'll drive.'

Carina agreed. It was Monday afternoon, a good day to visit because any new clients to the properties had settled in by then. Fortunately, there hadn't been any trouble with any of them, and Carina felt relaxed. It had been fun showing Annabel how she set about cleaning the properties when the clients had left. It was fun, too, chatting to them and waving them off after hearing about their holidays and all that they had done. Even Mr Blackett was happy after two weeks here and left looking years younger.

Ginny had left Thrift Cottage looking immaculate.

'A good family to have in,' Annabel said.

'Not what you would have thought when they first arrived,' Carina told her. 'Mr

Blackett, especially, was a nightmare.'

'Shows what good Cornish air can do,' Annabel said, as she signalled to turn left into the drive of Madrenna House.

As she did so, a car came out at speed, the man at the wheel seeming oblivious of them as he swept across their path. Carina had time to note his dark expression. 'Marcus!'

Shaken, Annabel drove in through the gates and pulled up. 'I wouldn't like to meet him on a dark night,' she said.

'Or at any other time, believe me,' Carina said.

They found Taryn in the conservatory on his own, leaning back in his chair with his eyes closed.

'Uncle'?' Carina said softly.

He opened his eyes. 'My dear!'

Carina smiled. 'I've brought my friend to see you.'

Taryn extended a frail hand and Annabel took it and held it in both of hers. Carina was concerned to see that today he looked tired and drawn. She wondered where his friend, Rosa Marshall, was.

They didn't stay long and on the way out Carina tapped on the door of the matron's office.

'I'll wait outside,' Annabel said.

Marcia Jolliffe greeted Carina with a smile. 'Come in, my dear. I was about to phone Mrs Trent. Mr Curnow, your uncle, is a little weak, but he always seems better for your visits.'

'He'll . . . be all right?' A stupid thing to say, but she couldn't help it.

'We're hoping so. He's a dear old man, but he is very elderly. He's got a lot of willpower, though, and that's a good thing. Don't worry too much, my dear.' She gave Carina a gentle pat on the arm.

'He's in the very best place,' Carina murmured.

The older woman smiled. 'We do all we can.'

Carina hadn't seen Jamie since before Annabel's arrival because they had people arriving late on Saturday, and afterwards, she had been too tired to think of going down to the weekly beach barbecue. On Sunday, he had been involved with some activity or other down near Penzance. She had missed him, though. He had phoned since then, eager to see her. He hadn't given up on her joining him at *Leapaway*, either. Laughingly, she told him that Annabel made her life at Spray Point too easy now to even consider doing anything else.

'I don't believe a word of it, not with a boss like Belinda,' he said. 'You'll find yourself out on your ear one of these days for some trivial reason, just like Zena.'

'Don't be so pessimistic,' she said, smiling.

'Optimistic, you mean. I want you for *Leapaway*, don't I?'

'So you say.'

'I'm serious, Carina. I'm still looking for good people. Tomorrow we've got two more applicants to see. We're taking them to Tullick to see how they shape up.'

'I hope it goes well. Don't drown them, will you? Anyway, our weekend went brilliantly. No complaints from the clients and everyone thinking they were in Heaven.'

'And so they are with you to look after them.'

'It's the view that does it every time.'

'Outside or inside?'

She laughed. 'They can't get over having a different view of the sea from every window.'

'That must be nice, certainly. By the way, we'll be making a night of it after our coasteering sessions next weekend, a sort of publicity session to put ourselves on the map. Zena's making huge plans. I'll let you know the details. Make sure you come, and bring that fabulous friend of yours I've heard so much about.'

'I won't be able to keep Annabel away.'

'There'll be a barbecue on the beach as usual, but at your end of it this time, for a change. Plenty of free parking for prospective clients.'

'You're expecting a crowd, then?'

'Free eats and drinks, and we've gone overboard on advertising.'

'You can't do any more than that,' Carina agreed.

His voice grew softer. 'And afterwards we'll escape somewhere, just you and me.'

She had a sudden vision of the two of them walking along the dunes as dusk was falling. The soft sand beneath their bare feet would still be warm from the sun that had shone on it all day. A faint breeze would rustle the marram grass as they moved among it to find a secret, beautiful place of their own, the sound of distant shouts and laughter fading into the distance. She thought of his eyes and the way his mouth felt on hers and the taste of his lips.

'See you there, then, Carina,' Jamie said, sounding so matter of fact, that she was immediately back in the present. She felt herself flush, as if he could see into her thoughts. Jamie filled them a lot these days as she acted out imaginary scenarios in which he took the leading role. Pure escapism of course, she thought now, as she returned to the kitchen to see about making a list of things to purchase for the apartments, and as unlikely to happen in real life as Annabel falling for Marcus and transforming him into a loveable romantic.

Marcus, she thought with a stab of

131

apprehension. For some reason she hadn't mentioned his brother to Jamie, not wanting to ruin their brief time together with talk of so unpleasant a man. In any case, she didn't think Jamie would have an explanation for his brother's odd behaviour.

Best to leave well alone.

A ROMANTIC EVENING

'Should I count the teaspoons?' Annabel asked next morning as she and Carina started on the cleaning of one of the apartments.

Carina laughed. 'If you think it's necessary. And while you're at it, make sure the dishwasher is emptied and that nothing's left in there. I'm making a start on the en suite.'

'You're a hard taskmaster.'

Her friend's rueful tones belied her enthusiasm about preparing the place for the next family arriving this afternoon. It was Annabel who had been up first this morning and had breakfast on the table.

Annabel was wearing shorts today and the skimpiest orange top Carina had yet seen. Her arms had caught the sun yesterday and she looked glowing. 'I can't wait to get going,' she had said.

And, once in the apartment, she had worked hard.

Belinda phoned when they were halfway through the cleaning. 'We've got a late booking for today, so put them in Marina Cottage, Carina, will you? The place needs a good clean. Do something about it immediately.'

'I'll have to go,' Carina said. 'Sorry, Annabel. Will you be all right here?'

'Of course I will,' Annabel said cheerfully.

'Trouble is, I haven't cleaned the grill and oven yet.' Carina opened the grill, took out the grill pan and recoiled in horror. 'Oh no! This will take ages.'

'Good thing I'm here to do it, then.'

She couldn't have managed today without Annabel, Carina thought, as she reversed the van out of its parking space to drive to Marina Cottage.

The state of the place was even worse than Belinda had indicated and it was well into the afternoon before she had finished the cleaning to her satisfaction. Her mobile rang as she replaced the cleaning materials in the cupboard on the landing. The family for the apartment had arrived in town and were inquiring about being able to get in early.

'That would be fine,' Carina told them. 'I'll be there to meet you in ten minutes.'

Hastily she changed into the clean white T-shirt she had brought with her. Belinda wouldn't thank her for meeting clients looking grubby and dishevelled. Her jeans weren't too

133

bad and would pass, thank goodness.

Parking nearby was out of the question, so she took advantage of the supermarket car park and walked the rest of the way to the apartment, at the same time phoning Annabel to tell her what was happening.

*   *   *

'What time do you call this?' Annabel said, when eventually Carina arrived back at Spray Point.

'This is our life from now on as we get busier,' Carina pointed out, as she picked up the sandwich her friend had prepared for her.

'You'll be passing out for lack of food. The rest of the afternoon off, what's left of it, wouldn't you say? I want to go down to the beach.'

'Off you go, then. I've got records to update on the computer and then I'll get ready to meet Jamie. That's not 'til eight, though. With luck, the Marina Cottage people will have arrived by then.'

Carina allowed herself another ten minutes' rest and then set to work. But Jamie's cheerful countenance kept swimming into her mind, however hard she tried to concentrate on the screen in front of her. Where was he at this moment; clambering round inaccessible cliffs, exploring dark caverns, or jumping into the water and bobbing about counting heads of the people in his charge? Not a bad way to earn a living. She stared dreamily at the keyboard, wishing she were doing the same. The cleaning today had been hard and Belinda seemed to expect even more of her now that Annabel was here to help.

Carina glanced at her watch. Where were the new clients? She had showered and changed by the time Annabel came back from the beach. Carina hated to ask, but she had to, if she didn't want to stand Jamie up.

'Don't worry about me,' said Annabel. 'You go and enjoy yourself and tell the gorgeous man from me that he's a lucky guy.'

Carina smiled. 'I'll make it up to you, I promise.'

'Just go,' said Annabel. 'A barbecue on the beach is the last thing I fancy at this present moment.'

'You don't sound too convincing.'

'There'll be other times.'

'You're a real mate,' said Carina. 'I'll leave my mobile. They'll phone when they get near and all you have to do is drive to Marina Cottage and let them in. Here are the keys. You're sure about this?'

Annabel picked up a towel and aimed it at her. 'Clear off before I change my mind.'

Laughing, Carina did as she was bid.

The evening was hazy and no wind stirred the surface of the sea as Carina made her way down to the beach. She could see the others already there and someone had lit a fire, although it wasn't yet dark.

Jamie saw her at once as she came down the steps and came running to greet her. He held her to him in a tight hug and then bent to kiss her. His lips tasted cool and salty.

'Some of the crowd are planning to go into town afterwards,' he said as he released her. 'But I declined for us. Was that all right?'

'Definitely all right,' Carina replied, smiling.

He stood back and gazed at her. 'You look beautiful tonight,' he said. Carina took a deep breath of pleasure, glad that she was wearing her floaty blue and white top with her white jeans and jewelled sandals and was carrying her navy fleece.

'Hey, Jamie, this is a publicity session, remember.' Zena's voice sounded playful, but Carina could see that there was something purposeful behind it.

Jamie waved his hand dismissively. 'All in good time.'

But the magic of the moment was broken.

More people were crowding down the steps now, laughing and talking. Several came up to the team, demanding to know what coasteering was all about. Others wandered around looking at the posters on the noticeboards stuck into the sand. Some picked up the leaflets from the pile on the plastic table and studied them.

'They all look interested,' Carina said.

'Looking isn't everything,' Jamie said. 'We need to get the food and drink on the go. I'll have to chivvy everyone up.'

*   *   *

'Need any help?' Carina asked Zena, who was busy organising a team of barbecue chefs who were wearing tall white hats and black wetsuits.

'We can cope,' said Zena shortly.

Feeling in the way, Carina picked up a leaflet. Someone had done a good job of setting out the aims of *Leapaway* with suitable illustrations of figures jumping off cliffs. It all looked intriguing. With luck, plenty of other people would think so, too, and want to sign on as instructors. Suitably qualified people, of course.

The evening wore on. Jamie was in the thick of it, obviously enjoying himself and oblivious of anything else except talking about his beloved project. She smiled at his enthusiasm.

After a while she took her paper plate of food and her mug of tropical fruit juice and found a place to sit on a sand dune from where she could look down on the proceedings. The noise from many voices rose into the night sky and the fire where the food was being cooked burned low and crimson. Someone had lit another fire of driftwood to provide light, and the flames from this rose. She could almost feel the heat from here and definitely smell the dry seaweed that had been thrown on as fuel. She pulled on her fleece and settled into a more comfortable position.

The food was good and Carina found she was hungry. She ate slowly, savouring every mouthful, wondering why food eaten in the open air always tasted better. She hoped Annabel was cooking herself something special. She deserved a good rest after the exhausting day they'd had.

Jamie was nowhere to be seen, no doubt busy convincing people what a good company *Leapaway* would be to work for. Or invest in. But his brother was going to do that, Jamie had said. Marcus was good for something, then. She leaned back against the sandy bank and closed her eyes.

*   *   *

'So here you are.'

Carina came to with a start. 'What's the time?'

'Pretty late.' Jamie threw himself down at her side, yawning. 'What a night! A success, I think. Yes, definitely. Several bookings, and two blokes and a girl interested in instructor training. Not a bad evening's work.'

Carina sat up and rubbed her eyes. The noise around the fires hadn't abated. Someone had brought a guitar and a few people were dancing on the sand, egged on by a raucous group cheering and shouting. She marvelled that she had actually slept through all this.

'Tired?' Jamie said.

'A bit.' She glanced at her watch. 'Nearly midnight,' she said in dismay. 'I've got to be up early tomorrow.'

Jamie sprang up. 'Me, too. A big group have booked for Tullick cliffs.' He put out a hand to help her up. 'I'll walk you home. I'll just tell Zena we're going.'

Carina followed Jamie down to the others and then, hand in hand, they walked across the sand to the steps. Neither spoke as they reached the top and started walking across the grass to the road. There were no lights on at Spray Point. No surprise there. Annabel would be as tired as she was herself and had obviously decided on an early night. Well, fairly early, Carina reminded herself.

They reached the uneven part of the road. To their right, the sea rolled in invisibly. Far away, the light on Trevose Head flickered. At the bottom of the steps up to Spray Point,

Jamie stopped and pulled her close. She melted into his arms.

'Tomorrow?' he said. 'I'll give you a buzz, okay?'

She sensed that he watched her until she opened the door, although it was too dark to see him.

The sound of the front door opening with a crash woke Carina next morning. She leapt out of bed, heart thudding, grabbed her fleece and pulled it on over her pyjamas with trembling hands. Annabel had heard the sound, too, and was already in the hall, rubbing her eyes and facing a furious Belinda.

'What's wrong?' Carina cried.

'What's wrong?' Belinda demanded. 'I was woken at two a.m., that's what's wrong, and had to get up and go to Marina Cottage and let the family in myself!'

Carina looked at her, bemused.

'They were *that* late?' Annabel said. 'Did they say why?'

Belinda's face reddened. 'I expect our clients to be treated with the utmost respect. What were they supposed to do at that hour of the morning?'

'Phone and say they were held up and would be arriving early today, instead?' Annabel suggested.

Belinda glared at her. 'I'll have no cheek from you.'

'You mean they didn't turn up until two o'clock in the morning?' said Carina. A cold feeling ran through her.

'That's exactly what I'm saying. Perhaps you'd tell me why you didn't know this?'

'I was on arrival duty from eight last night,' said Annabel, before Carina could reply. 'Carina needed time off. Much overdue, if I may say so. I stayed up till midnight and then went to bed. Reasonable, I thought.'

'Reasonable?' Belinda spat out. 'I say again, what were they supposed to do?'

'And I say again, book in somewhere else for the night. One of us being expected to stay up all night was far beyond the call of duty.'

For a moment Belinda was speechless, but then she turned to Carina. 'I employed you to do the job because I thought you were a responsible girl and could cope with all I expected from you.'

'A slave, more like,' Annabel muttered.

'That's enough!'

'I'm sorry,' Carina said. Had she been here, she could have got the details of the absent clients up on her computer and given them a call on their mobile. It wasn't Annabel's fault that she hadn't told her this.

'I can do without someone like your friend here being so obstructive and incompetent. You'll have to manage on your own, Carina, from now on. Pack your bags and go, Annabel, or whatever your name is!'

'That's not fair!' Carina burst out.

Belinda gave a grim smile. 'That's what the clients said when they got here tired and shocked after being held up for hours because of an accident.'

'They weren't injured?' said Carina in horror.

'No, thankfully.'

'So why didn't they phone Carina to tell her what had happened?' Annabel asked.

'Just get out,' snapped Belinda. 'And you, Carina, go round to Marina Cottage at once and apologise. Think yourself lucky that *you* still have a job.'

'Lucky?' cried Annabel but Belinda had already turned to go and the next moment was out of the door and striding down the steps.

*   *   *

'What a terrible woman,' Annabel said. 'I'll be glad to be out of here.'

'I don't blame you.'

'Oh, Carina, I didn't mean it. I've come down here to help you. I'll hide away somewhere so she won't know I'm here.'

Carina laughed, although she didn't feel like it. '*You* hide away, Annabel. I don't think so. And why should you, anyway?'

'Well, perhaps not. Since this is my holiday

and I don't exactly need the money, I'll find somewhere else to stay and give you a hand in secret.'

'Belinda's totally out of order,' Carina said. 'One slip up, that's all. No harm done, either, as she let them into the cottage. And she's so rude about you. It's not right to treat you like this. I don't need the money from Belinda's job to be near my great-uncle. Jamie wants me to work for him.'

'There you are then,' Annabel said.

'But I need somewhere to stay.'

'Then stay with me. I'm on holiday, remember, for two weeks, and then we'll think of something.'

Carina looked at her, considering. 'Well, yes . . .'

'Come on then, what are we waiting for?' Annabel said. 'I'm getting dressed and packed. We'll grab something to eat and then go.'

'I'll phone Belinda.'

'No way. Not till you're fixed up with Jamie.'

This seemed the best solution, Carina thought. In any case, she would have to be quick, or Jamie would be off somewhere with his group and she wouldn't know where to find him.

*　　　*　　　*

Zena was busy painting the *Leapaway* logo on the side of one of the vans when Carina and

Annabel got down to the usual parking spot near the beach. Totally absorbed in her task, Zena didn't look up at their approach. Carina watched her for a moment carefully outlining the lettering. 'A good design,' she said.

A drop of blue paint dropped to the ground as Zena's paintbrush shook. 'Now see what you've made me do.'

'It's great,' Carina said.

Slightly mollified, Zena dipped her brush in the paint again. 'You like it?'

'I thought you'd be with the others today. Jamie said you had a few bookings.'

'Someone else is having a go as instructor with Jamie this morning. He provided his own vehicle, so they didn't need the van.'

'Where can we find them?'

'Tullick Head.'

'Thanks, Zena. See you!'

'Where's Tullick Head?' Annabel asked as they went back to Spray Point for her car.

'Up the coast a bit. D'you mind driving me? You can drop me off there and go off flat hunting.'

'You're the boss.'

Carina set off swiftly along the cliff path towards the spot where the *Leapaway* people had worked from before. She could see Jamie gesticulating to a group of black-clad figures.

She would recognise him anywhere. She would also recognise the person beside him.

Rob.

A spasm of deep hurt ran through her. Rob? She couldn't believe it. So it was Rob who was the new instructor being put through his paces this morning. Why hadn't Jamie told her?

For an instant she froze. Then she turned and ran.

'Wait!'

Ignoring Rob's urgent call, Carina quickened her pace. Rob was with the *Leapaway* group, obviously a part of it. Rob was working for Jamie, who knew her reason for coming to Cornwall because she had told him, and yet he had gone ahead and employed Rob without telling her.

She couldn't work for Jamie now.

JAMIE ISSUES AN ULTIMATUM

'Stay right where you are,' Annabel said. 'I'll pick you up in twenty minutes.'

'Thanks.'

Carina looked about her, feeling the cooling breeze on her face. A grassy slope nearby provided a good place to wait for Annabel and she flopped down on the soft turf. From here she could gaze at the sea, grey today and reflecting the leaden sky. She sat with her hands clasping her knees and stared at the dismal scene while in her ears she still seemed to hear the echo of Rob's urgent shout.

'*Carina!*'

She had run faster along the narrow path, aware of the churning of the sea against the rocks down below.

Pounding footsteps had come swiftly up behind her. 'Carina! Don't run away!'

She had turned to face him, her cheeks burning. 'Rob?' To her own ears her voice sounded strangled and she took a deep gasping breath.

He looked like a stranger in the black wetsuit and orange buoyancy aid. 'Aren't you pleased to see me?' he said.

She didn't answer, merely said, 'What are you doing here?'

'*Leapaway* needed more staff. Coasteering's a new concept to me. I wanted to have a go.'

'Sadie?' she said roughly. 'What have you done about Sadie? Have you left her on her own?'

'For goodness' sake. Carina, what's got into you? The girl, Zena, assured me you were feeling homesick and would welcome a familiar face. Look, I'll have to get back.'

'Then go?'

'Carina, please . . .'

'You knew I wanted to come down here to Cornwall on my own. And why have you left

146

Sadie when she needs you?'

He caught hold of her. 'You've got a poor opinion of me if you think I'd do that.'

'Let me go!'

'Not until we get this straight.'

'But I still don't know why you're here.' She was almost sobbing now. 'There are other coasteering organisations. Why *Leapaway?*'

'Hey, you're really upset.'

'Rob, please . . .'

'Mum's in Woodbury at this very moment, being cosseted by those friends of hers.'

'But she didn't tell me.'

'A snap decision. A lot to do. They insisted they could look after her, so she didn't miss her bird-watching holiday. Satisfied?'

She pulled away, struggling to keep her composure. 'You're making this up.'

'Of course I'm not making it up!'

'So she sent you down here to check up on me?'

He released her, angry now. 'You're crazy. There's no getting through to you in this mood. I'll contact you later, okay?'

'No, it's not okay.'

'Didn't you know I'd applied for this job?'

'I suppose I did.'

'Well, then, why all the fuss? Zena said . . .'

She stood, poised for flight. 'How long are you here for?'

'As long as they'll have me.'

'What sort of answer is that?'

'What sort of answer do you want?'

'I . . . I don't know.'

Someone called his name.

'Coming!' he shouted.

She turned away, but still he didn't move. She heard the cry of seabirds, faint human voices. The moment seemed heightened by her distress. Only last night Jamie had begged her to come and work for him. Now this!

Feeling hurt and betrayed, she moved away so swiftly she caught her foot on a tree root and would have fallen if Rob hadn't caught her. For a moment he held her against him and she felt the coolness of the wet suit and the strength of his body. Somehow, in a way she couldn't understand, there was something comforting in the way he held her.

'I've got to go,' he murmured, releasing her. 'But we need to talk, Carina.'

*　　　*　　　*

'You look pale,' Annabel commented. 'Are you okay?'

Carina smoothed her hand over the bench inside the small caravan her friend had discovered to rent on a farm a few miles inland. From the outside, it looked in urgent need of a coat of paint, but the interior was spotless.

'It's a bit small,' Annabel admitted, 'but it'll do me, and you too if you want.'

148

Carina shook her head. 'I have to keep my job with Belinda now Rob's going to be working for *Leapaway*.' Suddenly she wanted to be back at Spray Point getting on with the life that had become familiar. There was Taryn to visit this afternoon, too. She mustn't forget that.

They drove back to Spray Point. The van was in the same position as when they had left and the front door still stuck in the same way and would only open with a strong push. Nothing had changed and yet, somehow, to Carina, everything was different.

Rob pushed open the door of the *Leapaway* van and emerged into the salty air of the harbour front. He took a deep breath, reminded of seaside holidays long ago and how he had revelled in the space and freedom after the confines of city streets. The freedom New Zealand had given him, too, was wonderful. He was beginning to feel the same here.

He could live in a place like this.

He'd had a good day with *Leapaway* and enjoyed every moment of the route they had taken round the base of the Tullick cliffs. He definitely had a good feeling about this new venture. Coasteering was a great idea and was catching on fast.

149

At the debriefing meeting, the young boss, Jamie Trent, had clapped him on the shoulder as he expressed his appreciation of his new employee, and that had been good to hear, too.

But now, standing here with the harbour sounds of boat engines and wheeling seagulls, he felt the need for something more to make life complete. He had returned from New Zealand intending to stay for good, feeling a certain need to be back in his own country. He had been at pains, though, to keep this to himself until he was quite certain he was making the right decision.

His mother had been good about his decision to leave three years ago, understanding his need to be in at the beginning of things on the other side of the world when the chance came. Now he wanted to be at home keeping a weather eye on her. He was aware, too, that she was deeply concerned about Carina. The bird-watching holiday and the *Leapaway* advertisement for staff provided the perfect excuse for coming down to Cornwall and checking on Carina before he decided finally on his future plans. His belongings were even now stored at a friend's house near Heathrow. He had promised to collect them as soon as he had made his final decision. And that must be soon.

He glanced round and saw that the door of

the stone building Jamie had told him was the old salt house stood wide open. He walked towards it, glad of the opportunity to look inside and see if it would be suitable for the headquarters of *Leapaway*.

The inside was airy and dry. Excellent. So, too, was the area of space that could be divided into smaller, more useful, rooms for storage, an office, and small lecture rooms set up with computers and projectors for demonstrations and briefings. Yes, this was the place, and Jamie had had the sense to see it. A fair amount of money would be needed for the purchase, of course, and for the alterations that would make it into the perfect venue.

For a second the doorway darkened. Rob moved forward so that the man who had entered could see who he was.

'Who are you and what do you want?' the man said sharply.

'I'm just taking a look.' Rob said pleasantly. 'This is a fine building.'

'Yes. I'd like to make an offer on it, but I'm waiting for the death of a very old man.'

For a startled second Rob froze, his eyes on the other man's face. 'I'm Rob Mason,' he said eventually.

'Marcus Trent.' He shot out his hand and shook Rob's. His grip was vice-like.

'So you are Taryn Curnow's great-nephew?' Rob said.

'May I ask how you know his name?'

Rob smiled. 'Ways and means.' He could see he had intrigued him, just as Marcus Trent had interested him with his remark about buying the salt house.

Marcus Trent's eyes narrowed. 'There's something here I don't understand.'

Rob shrugged. 'The door was open. I came inside.'

'And you're no longer welcome.'

'So it appears. No harm done, surely? It's a fine building. I take it you're connected in some way with Jamie Trent's coasteering business?'

'I don't know what my half-brother's been telling you, but the old man's my great-uncle, not his.'

'Why are you telling me this?'

'Please leave.'

At Madrenna Nursing Home, Carina was relieved to see that her great-uncle was looking less frail today and that the twinkle was back in his eyes. She smiled at the way he patted the seat at his side for Mrs Marshall to join them. Rosa was wearing pink this afternoon and settled back in her chair looking as if she expected to remain there for the rest of the day.

As perhaps she would, Carina thought. The old couple somehow looked so right together.

As Carina was leaving, Mrs Trent passed her at the front door and stopped. 'I do hope you haven't tired him. I'm not sure he should be having so many visitors. Has the matron said anything to you?'

'Only greeted me in her usual friendly way,' Carina said. But the welcome today had been slightly different, now she came to think of it. There had been something in Marcia Jolliffe's eyes, the same sort of twinkle as in Taryn's.

'I won't keep you,' said Mrs Trent, obviously anxious to get inside.

Carina emerged into a cloudy afternoon. A faint drizzle dampened the air and the surroundings looked dismal. She didn't doubt for a minute that Marcus would hear of her visit this afternoon. What would he do, knowing she had disobeyed his commands?

*   *   *

Back at Spray Point, there was more work to be done and Carina settled down to the records that needed updating. Belinda had phoned to tell her of more bookings, and her voice on the telephone had sounded friendly. There was no mention of Annabel's departure, or of finding more staff to help with the cleaning of the properties.

If only she had someone to share the workload at the busy times, Carina thought. Not to mention the occasions when she had to be in several different locations at once, or when, as was apparent now, she had to be prepared to stay up all night in case someone was late in arriving.

Sighing, she got up from the computer and went to the window. The roar of the sea was always there, but now she could hardly see it because of the mist that had come rolling in, obliterating everything. She wondered if the coasteering group were back yet. Surely they couldn't do much in these conditions?

The phone rang.

'Get round to Heather Cottage, Carina,' Belinda said, her voice brisk. 'An emergency. I'm at the hospital. I said you'd be there at once.'

'What kind of emergency?' Carina said.

The silence on the other end was deafening, because Belinda had rung off.

At Heather Cottage, the clients' parking space was empty. The cottage door flew open and the young mother stood there, her child in her arms. The long skirt she was wearing dragged on the ground and Carina could see that her feet were bare.

'Is something wrong, Mrs Davenport?' asked Carina.

'Susie. Come in.'

The passage to the big open plan room was

full of cases and bags and looked as if a panic-stricken elephant had run amok.

'Sorry it's a bit of a mess,' Susie said. 'I'm supposed to be finishing the unpacking while Harry's away, but Zeppelin fell over in the garden and hurt his knee. Now he won't let me put him down.'

'Zeppelin?' said Carina, looking at the child. 'So that's the problem . . . ?'

'Oh no,' said Susie quickly. 'It's my husband, Harry. He hasn't come back.'

'Where did he go?'

'This thing called coasteering,' Susie said helplessly. 'He's been gone hours. He booked the session on the Internet at home. I didn't want him to go. Not in this mist. But it was so pricey he didn't want to cancel and lose the money.'

Zeppelin was asleep on his mother's shoulder now, a thumb in his mouth.

'He's with *Leapaway?* He's bound to be all right, Susie. Please don't worry.'

Susie stood drooping in distress. 'But he's taken the mobile.'

'There's no signal here, anyway,' Carina said. It was too bad of Harry going off and leaving everything to his poor young wife. 'I can easily check he's safe by phoning the instructor from the best point for picking up a signal near here,' she suggested to the distraught young woman.

Susie brightened. 'You can?'

155

'Of course. I'll be right back.'

Jamie answered at once. Harry Davenport had completed today's course and should now be on his way home, as he'd chosen to use his own car.

'I see,' Carina said. 'Thanks.'

'A problem?'

'Could be.'

But even before she had put her phone back in her pocket, a red car swept round the corner and screeched to a stop. She recognised Susie's young husband at once.

He wound down his window. 'Good to see you again,' he said cheerfully.

'Susie's frantic because you're late,' Carina said.

'I got lost,' he said, unrepentant. 'No harm done.'

Except to his wife's peace of mind, Carina thought, as he drove on. Her legs felt weak with the worry of it all, followed by the huge relief at finding that Harry Davenport was safe.

To her surprise, the *Leapaway* van drove up then and stopped. Jamie leaned across and wound down the window on the passenger side. 'Everything okay?'

'Oh, Jamie,' Carina said.

He pushed open the door. 'Get in.'

She did so. 'My van's parked round the corner.'

'You can get it later.' His voice sounded

grim. He looked different too, his mouth unsmiling. He yanked the van into gear and reversed swiftly before driving away at speed.

'What's the matter?' Carina said.

'You solved the problem with young Davenport?'

'He's just got back. It was good of you to come, Jamie,' she said. 'I was so afraid of an accident.'

He made no reply.

'Where are we going?'

'Somewhere we can talk.'

They were out in the main road now, driving towards Spray Point.

'Why didn't you tell me Rob's going to be working for you?' she said.

'Well . . . Zena said not to.' He sounded evasive.

She said no more as he pulled in to the side of the road where the surfers parked to get down the steps to the beach.

He pulled on the hand brake and turned to face her. 'I've just had bad news,' he said. 'Marcus has issued an ultimatum. He'll withdraw his financial backing of *Leapaway* immediately unless you promise never to visit the old man in the nursing home again.'

Carina looked at Jamie in horror. 'But he can't do that!'

Jamie gave a bitter laugh. 'Oh yes, he can. It would be the end of *Leapaway*, believe me.'

For a moment this was impossible to take

in. Then Carina became aware of an iciness creeping down her spine. Jamie was serious.

'You want me to give up visiting Madrenna Nursing Home?' she said in disbelief.

He stared ahead at the line of parked vehicles. 'I don't see any alternative. Marcus means what he says.'

She gazed at him, her mind whirling. 'But why?'

'Why does Marcus do anything?' Jamie said bitterly, 'except to suit himself. I know that. We all know that. But it makes no odds in the long run. He's got the upper hand here.'

'But why should it matter to Marcus who I visit or don't visit?'

'Oh it matters, believe me.'

'But I don't understand.'

'It matters to my brother if there's money involved.'

Carina gazed at the dashboard in front of her, thinking hard. Marcus believed she was here only to worm her way into the old man's affections. He had already tried to warn her off because he suspected Taryn was going to change his will in her favour. But what did that matter to Marcus?

She turned to look at Jamie. His profile appeared carved in stone. She had never seen him like this before. She wanted the old Jamie back, happy and carefree and bursting to tell her all the plans he was making for the success of *Leapaway*. But it wasn't going to be like that any more unless she agreed to do as Marcus wanted. And, it was crystal-clear that's what Jamie wanted, too.

'I need to think,' she said.

He nodded. 'Bear in mind it's an old man we're talking about here who can't have much longer to live. It's the future we have to think about now. And people's livelihood. Don't be selfish, Carina.'

'I must go,' she said, her voice low.

He made no move to stop her and that alone spoke volumes.

Seagulls called in the distance and the air felt good on her face but she was in no mood to appreciate it. All that filled her mind was Jamie asking her not to see Taryn again. He had told her not to be so selfish. But he wouldn't have said that if he knew of her great-uncle's pleasure in her company, the way his eyes lit up when she walked in, and the promise she had made to him that she would come to see him again. Was she to break that promise now, because of the ultimatum Marcus had issued? And would she even have the chance to explain it to Taryn before the ban clamped down on her?

Jamie believed his brother was serious, and she must believe it, too.

The surfers were still out in the bay but the

surf had died away and the sea was calm. Carina saw one of the hopefuls standing up on his board closely followed by the others doing the same thing and allowing the incoming tide to move them slowly towards the beach. They looked strange, like seals floating on the water.

At any other time she would have stood and watched, but now she continued on her way, deep in thought. How would Taryn possibly understand if her visits suddenly stopped? He had made it plain that she meant as much to him as he did to her. He was her blood relation and dear to her because of it. Jamie's friendship was dear to her, too, but it would be all over if she didn't agree to his request. *Leapaway* was his dream. She knew he needed his brother's financial input to be able to make his business the success he wanted.

She reached the bottom of the steps before she remembered the van she had left parked near Heather Cottage. There was nothing for it but to retrace her steps to collect it.

CARINA MAKES A DECISION

Seated at the kitchen table with both hands wrapped round her coffee mug, Carina continued to think long and hard. Jamie knew that his brother meant what he said and although he also was aware of how much visiting her great-uncle meant to her, he was asking her to give Taryn up for *Leapaway*'s sake. Could she do this?

Her mind sent pictures reeling in front of her eyes as if they were on a television screen. She saw black-clad figures feeling their way round rocky outcrops, swimming awkwardly in bulky buoyancy aids, vanishing into caves and enjoying themselves hugely as they took part in an activity of a lifetime. She saw Zena's bent head as she concentrated on painting the logo on the side of the van and Jamie's enthusiastic smile as he told her how much all this meant to him.

But there would be no future for *Leapaway* unless she agreed to stop her visits to her great-uncle. Taryn had Rosa now, who was a good friend to him, so maybe her absence wouldn't have the impact on the old man it might otherwise have done.

It would have an impact on her, though.

She became aware of the ringing of the telephone in the front room and got unsteadily to her feet.

Annabel's voice seemed to fill the room. 'How's it going then, Carina?' she said loudly, against a background noise of talk and laughter. 'I expected to hear from you before now.'

'Oh yes, sorry.'

'You sound odd. What's been happening?'

'A problem to sort out at Heather Cottage,

and then . . .'

'I can't hear you with all this racket going on. D'you want to join me? I've found this great place in town. We could eat here and . . .'

'I can't,' Carina said. 'I'll explain tomorrow, Annabel. D'you mind?'

'Won't have to, will I?' said Annabel cheerfully. 'Second best to the wonderful Jamie, is that it?'

Carina mumbled something and put the phone down. She wished she felt able to confide in her friend but this was something she had to work out for herself. Time enough to tell her when she knew herself what she was going to do.

Taking a sip of cooling coffee, Carina put the mug down again. A heart-wrenching decision had to be made and she must make it soon. 'Oh Taryn,' she murmured, a lump beginning to form in her throat.

*   *   *

She wished Sadie were here. Her loving support would be invaluable and she would understand how Carina's heart ached at her distress if she were forced to stop her visits to Taryn.

And yet . . .

Her refusal to do this thing he asked of her would hurt Jamie deeply. Could she do this to him?

162

Suddenly it was too much. She put her head in her hands and wept.

Rob strode to the tip of the headland and stood gazing down at the whirling water around the rocks at the base of the cliff and then he looked back at the distant beach. He could just make out the two *Leapaway* vans parked in their usual place, ready to set off again tomorrow with a new group of hopefuls anxious to take part in coasteering. How much better for them if there was a permanent building with changing rooms, showers and all the amenities a project like this demanded.

Yesterday, one or two of the clients had needed extra help in negotiating a couple of difficult scrambles and had been grateful for the attention he had given them and he had felt privileged to be there, knowing that his expertise was valuable to others. He definitely had a good feeling about this new venture. Helping to set up *Leapaway* and introducing more activities would provide the challenge he needed.

But to make a real go of it, *Leapaway* must be less amateurish.

He picked up a small stone and aimed it at a protruding rock down below. Bouncing off, it fell into the sea with a splash. He did it again and again until, tiring of the activity, he turned away. Jamie and the others had invited him to join them this evening at a newly-opened place in town, where food was served at huge tables outside. You were expected to stay for hours making as much noise as you liked as you watched the sun go down over the sea. Maybe he'd go there after all, even though it hadn't appealed at first.

He set off back across the flowery turf of the headland until he reached the narrow rutted road back to the *Leapaway* van to pick up his jacket. There were houses on the high ground to his right. Not a bad place to live, he thought, with that magnificent view up the coast. One of the properties had a newly-painted sign on the wall at the bottom of a flight of steps. Spray Point.

He looked up and saw a low white bungalow staring back at him. Spray Point. Carina's place. On sudden impulse he leapt up the steps and tapped on the door.

Carina heard the tap and then the sound of the door opening. The next moment Rob was in front of her. She looked up at him, warmth unaccountably flooding her face.

'I was passing,' he said abruptly.

She nodded and looked down at her hands clenched in her lap. 'I've a decision to make,' she said. 'A big one?'

'A problem?' He pulled out a chair from the table, turned it round and sat straddled on it with his arms resting on the back. 'D'you want to tell me about it, Carrie?'

'I found my great-uncle,' she said, with a sob in her voice. 'He's a dear old man. He was pleased to see me.'

Rob leaned forward. 'But surely that's good?'

'Of course it is. It's wonderful. And I can't give him up now.' She took a deep gasping breath. 'I'm not going to stop seeing him.'

Rob moved nearer. 'Does he want you to?'

'He's important to me, you see . . .' She broke off.

'But why should you stop seeing him?'

She reached for a tissue. '*Leapaway* will fold if I don't.'

He stared at her in obvious surprise and she struggled for breath as she explained. 'It's Marcus, Jamie's brother. He thinks I'm after money, the estate, and am worming my way into Taryn's affections so he'll leave it all to me. But I'm not. I don't want any part of it. I want to visit Taryn, that's all.'

'And?'

'Marcus will stop financing *Leapaway* unless I promise not to see my great-uncle again.'

She looked up and saw that Rob's brow was furrowed. 'So Marcus has a financial stake in the company? I might have guessed.'

'Jamie needs him to keep *Leapaway* going. He knows Marcus means what he says. Oh, Rob, I don't want to stop visiting Taryn. But Jamie . . .'.

'Jamie, Marcus Trent's brother?'

She nodded. 'So different from Marcus. But you know what Jamie's like.'

Rob was silent for a moment. 'Jamie Trent has creative imagination,' he said finally. 'This is his life's dream, and without it, he'll be nothing.'

She nodded, agreeing with every word. 'Jamic isn't afraid I'll stcal any inheritance,' she said. 'He's never even mentioned it.'

'Well, no, he wouldn't have, since it doesn't affect him.'

'What do you mean?' Carina said, puzzled.

'They share the same father, that's all. It's Marcus who's related to Taryn Curnow through his mother.'

'*Marcus* is related to my great-uncle?'

'Taryn's his great-uncle, too. His mother, Sarah, Mrs Trent, is the daughter of Taryn's sister, who died some years ago. Your grandfather's sister, too, of course. Marcus told me some of this yesterday when we met in the old building down by the harbour. I checked the rest out with Jamie. It's true, I assure you.'

She took a deep breath. 'So I'm related to Marcus and Mrs Trent. And that's why Marcus is so afraid of Taryn changing his will in my favour.'

'Distant relatives only,' Rob said, 'but family all the same.' His voice was low and she had to strain to hear him. 'But not Jamie. He means a

166

lot to you?'

She nodded.

He got up. 'That's what I thought.'

The next moment the room was empty. He was gone.

Her mobile rang into the silence. Carina did nothing in the hope that it would stop and leave her in peace. But whoever was on the other end didn't give up easily. She flicked her phone open.

Jamie.

Of course it was Jamie. He would be wanting to know if he could notify his brother that in future all communication between Carina and her great-uncle, Marcus's great-uncle, too, she reminded herself, would cease.

His voice sounded faint. 'I need to know, Carina. I'm seeing Marcus in an hour. What do I tell him?'

'I'm so sorry, Jamie,' she whispered. 'I can't do it. I can't give up visiting my great-uncle.'

'We need to talk some more, Carina, and quickly.'

'It's no use,' she said despairingly.

'But you know we need to have a permanent base, or we won't be able to function for much longer.'

'But why is Marcus in such a hurry with his ultimatum?'

'That's Marcus for you. He likes things cut and dried.'

She was silent. Marcus must obviously know

that Taryn had done nothing yet about changing his will, but feared he would do so in the near future in her favour. Did Jamie realise this? She was afraid to ask.

'Carina, are you still there?'

'I'll have to go now,' she said hopelessly.

'Please Carina, will you come to the *Surge and Swell* with me tomorrow night? A crowd of us will be there.'

'Marcus?'

'Not Marcus. You know it's not his scene.'

'I'll . . . I'll try to be there, Jamie.' Suddenly she felt drained. She wasn't even sure she wanted to see Jamie. All she wanted was some time on her own to assimilate all that had been happening in the last few hours.

But an undisturbed period of time was not an option, because she had to phone Belinda and report on the the bookings. Tomorrow there was a trip to the Cash & Carry and another load of sheets and duvet covers to wash.

She felt exhausted just thinking about it.

Next afternoon, Carina felt Annabel's awed gaze on her as they leaned on the balustrade high above the harbour. Sunlight glinted on the masts of the boats tied up by the harbour wall.

'You actually told the dreaded Marcus

168

exactly where to get off?' Annabel said.

'Hardly.' Carina smiled. She would never have had the courage to do that face to face.

'As good as!' Annabel said. 'So now what?'

Down below them, two young boys were manoeuvring a dinghy on its launching trolley down the slipway. Carina watched as it was taken into the water and the boat floated off. One of the boys stood knee-deep holding the boat while the other parked the trolley over by the wall and then joined his companion. They clambered in and set the sail before moving off towards the open sea.

'I never thought you had it in you,' Annabel was saying.

'D'you think I've made the right decision, though, Annabel? It wasn't easy.'

'Of course it was the right decision. You couldn't let rat-bag Marcus win.'

'But it means Jamie will lose out.' Carina shuddered. The pain of knowing that tore at her still.

'It's his problem, having a brother like Marcus.'

'I couldn't discard my great-uncle.'

'That dear old man? I should think not, now you've found him. When will you see him again? Aren't you due some time off?'

'That's what I'm having now, meeting you. Carina felt a strong need to confide in her friend, now she had decided on her course of action. This was a good place to do it, away from Spray Point, now the washing was blowing on the line in the wind and there was nothing more to do for the moment.

Annabel spun round, her face alight. 'Let's go to see Taryn now.'

Carina smiled. 'A woman of action. So what have you been doing with yourself since I saw you last?'

Annabel's cheeks dimpled as she smiled, too. 'Need you ask? All those surfers, not to mention the lifeguards!'

'Anyone in particular?'

'Might be. Dave comes from upcountry, near Reading. He's down here for a couple of weeks. He's really something, Carina, and . . . ' Annabel broke off, her eyes dreamy. 'We're meeting tonight at the *Surge And Swell*.'

'That's where Jamie wants to meet me, too.'

'So it's still on then? Good for you. The withdrawal of funds won't have kicked in yet, will it? You'll have to hope *Leapaway* gets lots of clients in the next few weeks and can do without Marcus.'

'It won't work like that. Jamie has an option on that old building over there, an old salt house, apparently It's perfect for *Leapaway* because of the location. The price is high because it's in a prime position and someone else is after it, too. Jamie's got until the weekend to clinch the deal and he can't do it without his brother. The council only agreed to him running the business from the vans for

170

a limited period.'

'Let's leave all this for now,' Annabel said. 'We can go and visit your great-uncle. My car's just up there.'

'Okay,' said Carina, taking a last look down below. The sailing dinghy with its crew of two was well away from the harbour now, its red sails billowing in the wind.

DANGER ON THE CLIFFS

Somehow this visit to Madrenna Nursing Home felt like a trial, Carina thought, as if she was testing the water for further visits in the face of Marcus's disapproval.

She pushed open the wide door. It felt good to be here again and to see Taryn in his usual chair in the conservatory. Annabel decided to drive on an exploring mission after dropping Carina, arranging to return to pick her up again in about an hour. 'You need time alone with the old man,' she said.

'My dear,' Taryn said with pleasure, as Carina approached. She bent to kiss him. 'How are you, Uncle?'

'Blooming,' he said.

He certainly looked it, she thought, as she drew up a chair and sat down.

'Rosa will be here in a few minutes,' he said. 'She's gone to telephone her son with our news.'

'News?' said Carina with interest.

He put out a gnarled hand to cover hers. 'I'll know you'll be pleased for us, my dear.'

Rosa came in then, smiling and bright-eyed. 'So Taryn has told you?' she said, as Carina leapt up to pull a chair forward for her.

'Not yet.'

'Then I shall have that pleasure.' She looked fondly at Taryn. 'Your uncle and I have decided to marry.'

Carina looked from one to the other in delight. 'That's wonderful! I couldn't be more pleased for you! I shall have a great-aunt as well as a great-uncle now.'

Rosa bent forward to give her a kiss. 'Apart from my son, you are the first to know my dear,' she said.

Taryn's eyes twinkled and he looked full of mischief. 'Can you keep our secret?'

'Of course she can,' said Rosa, looking at Carina fondly. 'She's a dear girl, your great-niece. Unlike some. We don't want anyone else to know until all the arrangements are in place. Of course, we shall tell Marcia, the Matron here, that's only right and proper. But I've an inkling she might have guessed already.'

This turned out to be the case when Marcia Jolliffe came in to offer coffee and cakes. When she had brought them she seated herself, and the rest of Carina's visit was spent in talk of weddings.

'We're giving ourselves four weeks to get organised,' Rosa said. 'Of course, we shall have the reception here in the grounds if the weather's kind to us. You see, dear, most of our friends are here and our families can be accommodated nearby.'

'You will come and support an old man, won't you, Carina my dear?' Taryn said, leaning forward in his chair.

Carina looked at his eager face. He seemed at least ten years younger. Smiling, she assured him that she would.

'I'm a lucky man,' he said. Rosa smiled at him and took his hand in hers.

They were so happy together it was a joy, and the hour sped swiftly. Carina bent to kiss both of them as she got up to go.

Taryn tapped the side of his nose. 'Don't forget what you promised, my dear.'

'I won't,' she said, smiling at him.

*   *   *

Sworn to secrecy as she was, Carina found it hard not to blurt out the good news to Annabel, but she managed, with difficulty, to keep it to herself. She wondered that her friend didn't notice the way she kept grinning as she thought of Rosa and her great-uncle together.

They parted, promising to be in touch very

soon, and Carina sprinted up the steps to Spray Point, feeling more light-hearted than when she had descended them only an hour or two before, after putting yet another load of sheets into the washing machine.

All the time she was hanging these out on the line now, she thought of her great-uncle and Rosa's happiness and of the plans they were making for their future life together. This altered everything, of course, rendering Marcus' ultimatum to her meaningless because Taryn would have to make a new will on his marriage anyway.

Carina woke late the next day, knowing at once that something was different. The roaring of the sea was muted and when she sprang out of bed to pad across to the window, nothing could be seen for the fog that shrouded everything.

This was a change in the weather that hadn't been forecast. *Leapaway* would be grounded, of course, with the resulting loss of income. No-one could go clambering about the cliffs in this. It would be highly dangerous.

She could just make out some of the jagged rocks on this side of the beach, but in the white gloom they looked strange and ghostly. She shivered, wishing the fog would go away and leave everything clear and bright, as it should be on an early June morning.

Her phone rang as she finished eating her breakfast.

'We've a problem,' a hesitant voice told her. 'I'm sorry to trouble you.'

'A problem?' she said.

'The door into the back garden seems to have got stuck. We can't open it.'

She let out a breath of relief that it was no worse. 'Thrift Cottage? I'll come right away.'

She grabbed her jacket, opened the door of Spray Point, and went out into the foggy air. She could see well enough to get down the steps, and found that the fog wasn't as bad as she had thought. The sea was visible now . . . just. A disembodied voice called through a loud hailer, making her jump.

'Stay with your boards,' it ordered. 'Look for the yellow life raft. It'll guide you in.'

The voice was still calling through the fog as Carina walked down and then along the road and she marvelled that any surfer would have ventured out in this. But perhaps they had been up early before the fog thickened.

The Thrift Cottage problem was soon sorted out, and by the time she left, the fog was beginning to lift.

To her surprise, the *Leapaway* van drove round the corner as she reached the main road.

Jamie leaned out of the open window. 'Want to come with us, Carina, and act as lookout? We've got a new instructor now, a chap called Tony, who's well qualified. We're going coasteering after all, a few miles up the coast from Tullick where there are some good caves.'

He sounded his old friendly self. Making an instant decision, she climbed in and sat beside him, and as they drove, he explained that the first *Leapaway* van was already there with the advance party. 'No fog up there,' he said, 'We're lucky.'

She was lucky, too, that he had invited her to go with them. Rob would be there, she thought, and then wondered why that should matter to her. She wondered, too, how many more chances like this there would be to watch Jamie at his coasteering work if Marcus had his way.

From her position on the clifftop, Carina had a panoramic view of everything going on below. The ten members of the first group were already in the water and now, one behind the other, were clambering over a line of rocks that would be submerged at high tide. Zena was in the lead in a blue buoyancy aid and Rob was at the back, similarly clad. Jamie led the second group that contained, to her surprise, Annabel. It was obvious that the man next to her was her new friend, Dave the surfer.

Bringing up the rear was the instructor, Tony. He, too, was wearing a blue buoyancy aid to distinguish him from the clients.

Carina watched anxiously as Annabel joined the others in the water with a squeal of excitement. Dave, shouting encouragement, was soon with her and together they got in line.

The leader, Zena, had reached the far end of the line of rocks and now each person had to negotiate a rush of water that carried them swiftly towards the base of the cliff. How would Annabel manage this? Easily, with Dave's help, as it turned out. No problem there.

The members of the first group were clambering round the base of the cliffs to reach the cave Jamie had told Carina was on the planned route. She watched each person vanish inside in turn.

She checked on the progress of the second group and then raised her eyes to where the horizon should be and saw to her dismay that it had disappeared into the mist. And so had the headlands further north. The fog was returning.

Hastily she reached in the pocket of her jeans for the whistle Jamie had given her and blew a long blast.

He looked up and waved but he was obviously already aware of the situation. The members of the second group were coming back the way they had started out, led by the other instructor. One or two had difficulty in climbing the cliff but at last they reached the top in safety. Annabel climbed as if she had been doing this all her life and laughed at Carina's expression as she joined her.

'That was great, wasn't it, Dave?' she said. 'Too bad we had to come back.'

He pulled off his helmct. 'Safety precautions,' he said, grinning at Annabel. 'Can't be too careful now visibility's deteriorating fast.'

But where was the first group? Until they emerged from inside the cave they wouldn't be aware of the fog creeping across the sea in swathes of white. She saw Jamie now, edging his way towards the cave entrance, and at last some figures came out to start on the torturous route back.

Carina glanced at Tony and saw that he was preparing to go to them, obviously believing his help might be needed. Dave urged everyone to keep well away from the cliff edge that any minute might vanish into the fog.

'It's okay, they're coming,' someone shouted.

Carina watched with a clutch of fear in her throat. Jamie was the last one up, but where was Rob? She clutched Jamie's arm. 'One's missing,' she said.

'Zena?'

A quick glance told her that he was right.

'Rob too,' she said, a tremor in her voice.

'I'm going back down,' he said, his voice tight. 'Coming, Tony?'

*   *   *

Carina was the official lookout and had her mobile out ready, in case the order came to alert the emergency services. She watched as Jamie and Tony made their way down the cliff. They were at the bottom now and she could just make out their shapes.

Shouts faded into the foggy silence. Then there were more calls and she strained to listen. She strained as well to see something in the oppressive whiteness. Figures loomed. They were coming . . . four of them.

Five minutes at the most had passed. But she felt as if she had lived five long days.

Tony appeared first, rising out of the gloom as he struggled up to the top of the cliff and then turned to help the next person, who was closely followed by Jamie. Carina rushed to help and saw that Zena, limp and exhausted, couldn't have managed the climb without help from the others.

She collapsed on the grass.

'Get her away from the edge,' Jamie said thickly.

Carina helped the others move her, fear in her heart. Something had happened down there. Jamie's face as be bent over Zena was

179

white and drawn. She opened her eyes and struggled to a sitting position. His arms were round her at once. 'Wait, Zena . . . rest. You'll be all right in a minute.'

She gazed back at him. 'Jamie?' He gently kissed her forehead.

At once Carina was aware she shouldn't be witnessing this private moment. Oddly enough, seeing Jamie and Zena together, like this, didn't affect her as much as she thought it would.

She turned away and waited for Rob to appear out of the thinning fog, fears for his safety uppermost in her mind. The sea was becoming visible now, headlands appearing where a minute ago white gloom had prevailed.

Rob had been some way behind the others and now she saw him begin the climb, shards of stones and loose soil falling away as he did so. She waited. He seemed to have come to no harm down there on the rocks but she had to be sure.

She stood back as he reached the top.

'Zena?' he said. 'Is she okay?'

'I'm fine,' said Zena, on her feet now but leaning against Jamie.

'What happened?' Tony said.

'I slipped,' Zena said. 'We could feel the fog from inside the cave and we heard Jamie's shouts. But I couldn't move. My foot was caught in something . . . Rob stayed to help. I thought we were done for.'

'We'd best get you home and get that injured foot looked at,' Jamie said. 'Come on, all of you. The day's activities are postponed.'

Zena took off her helmet and shook out her dark hair. Rob moved to her and gave her a hug. 'You're a brave girl. I'm proud of you.'

Carina felt a stab of . . . of what? as she witnessed this. Jealousy? Surely not.

With dragging steps, she followed the others to the vans. The last time they had been together Rob had seen that she had been crying. Now he didn't even glance in her direction, though he must have seen her standing there. She felt strangely hurt and alone.

The fog was vanishing now and light glimmered on the water out to sea.

'Hurry up, Carina, what are you waiting for?' Annabel called.

At Carina's feet, a clump of sea pinks that had been battered into the damp grass by uncaring feet, looked forlorn.

She bent to rescue one of them and held it to her, drinking in the delicate damp scent. She didn't know why she was waiting, because there was nothing for her here now. She walked slowly towards the nearest van.

A DEVASTATING PHONE CALL

'You know about the celebrations when we get back, don't you?' Annabel said, as Carina clambered into the van beside her. 'Jamie's been telling us. We've all got to get into our glad rags for a momentous announcement, he says. I can't wait.'

'Celebrations?

'At the *Surge And Swell.* He's just been on to them to lay something special on for the whole lot of us. He's got something to celebrate, but Dave won't tell me what it is.'

Carina glanced at Dave, who ran his hand through his damp auburn hair and grinned at her. No wonder Annabel liked him. He was good fun to be around and a good team worker, too.

Annabel gave Dave a friendly thump. 'Come on, Dave. Out with it. No secrets here.'

Still grinning, he retaliated in the same way, until Annabel squealed for mercy. 'Jamie wants to announce the good news himself,' he said.

Good news? Carina looked at Dave enquiringly. The only good news she knew about was Taryn and Rosa's forthcoming marriage. Hardly that, surely? Jamie would hardly be celebrating the loss of his brother's financial expectations and she wasn't sure that

Marcus knew about that, either. No, it was more likely a celebration of his new relationship with Zena.

'I'll have to give it a miss,' she said. 'Work at Spray Point calls.'

'Dreary nonsense,' Annabel said firmly. 'Come on, live a bit, why don't you, Carina?'

But Carina was firm. Jamie had invited her along this morning as a goodwill gesture to show he held no hard feelings and that was generous of him. But she wasn't part of *Leapaway*, either as a client or an instructor.

'You're not coming, Carina?' Jamie said in obvious disappointment as they spilled out of the vans back at the harbour. Zena, standing next to him, smiled.

Carina turned away and left them to it as they changed out of their wetsuits and chatted about the forthcoming lunch at the *Surge And Swell*. She felt hurt and alone and heart-sore. For Jamie? No, not for Jamie. Then for who . . .

'An unknown benefactor,' Annabel said jubilantly on the phone a couple of hours later. 'Can you believe it? Jamie's made up, I can tell you. Grinning from ear to ear, and Zena and he did a jig on one of the tables when we'd cleared all the food away. It was fantastic. You should have been there.'

183

'So who is this benefactor?' Carina wanted to know.

'I told you, no-one knows, but it means that Jamie can go ahead and buy that old place he wants.'

'The old salt house?'

'That's the one. And there'll be money left after that, too. It's all got to be signed and sealed, but Jamie's pretty sure it'll all go through without a hitch.'

'So *Leapaway*'s safe?' Relief flooded through Carina. So Marcus had had a change of heart and agreed to invest in *Leapaway* after all. 'I'm really delighted,' she said.

'I knew you would be. The lunch was fantastic and now there's to be a barbecue on the beach tonight as well. Fireworks, I shouldn't wonder. You'll come to that?'

'Of course.' It would be good to congratulate Jamie and show him her delight in his good fortune. He would have his dream now. 'See you there, then,' Annabel said as she rang off.

Carina stood at the window for a minute or two, letting her satisfaction flood through her. *Leapaway* would have a permanent base and Jamie could continue his work. She wished him well.

Annabel had already hinted that Dave would like to join *Leapaway.* Somehow, Carina suspected that her friend's future might be tied up in the business, too.

184

But what of her? What of her future?

Carina felt too unsettled to busy herself with computer work after lunch. Instead, she drove to Madrenna Nursing Home and parked the van in the gravel drive next to a four-by-four she hadn't seen before. Brand new, she noticed, its dark blue paintwork immaculate. It wasn't often that such an imposing vehicle turned up here.

Something was different inside the house, too, a brooding atmosphere she hadn't felt on other visits.

Marcia Jolliffe's face looked slightly drawn as she emerged from her office to greet her. 'There's been an upset,' she said.

Carina was alarmed. 'My great-uncle . . .'

'He's quite well, my dear,' Marcia said. 'There's nothing to worry about now. Your great-uncle's solicitor is with him at the moment and the other visitor has now left, I'm glad to say. I'm sure Mrs Marshall would like to see you in her room until your uncle is free.'

'Of course,' Carina said.

Rosa's room on the ground floor was papered with pink rosebuds on a white background and her furniture was white. She rose to greet her guest with a smile.

'What a pretty room,' Carina said.

Rosa looked pleased. 'Come and sit down,

dear. I was hoping to have a few words with you. Taryn is a little upset, but he'll be so pleased to see you once his business is done.'

It wasn't hard to guess the reason for the strange atmosphere. 'Has Marcus been to see him?' Carina asked anxiously.

Rosa frowned. 'So unpleasant and so uncalled for. Fortunately, the solicitor was already here with your uncle so this man, Marcus, couldn't do much. And it won't change anything. He knows that. And have you received your wedding invitation too, dear?'

Carina smiled. 'Not yet.'

'We made a start, you see. Marcus came threatening all sorts of terrible things as soon as he received his. Very upset, I'm afraid. I was so proud of Taryn for standing up to him and not allowing himself to be bullied.'

'I'm proud of him too,' Carina said.

Rosa leaned forward and patted Carina's arm. 'And now we need to ask you for a few addresses, dear.

'We want to invite that lovely lady who brought you up, and her son, and that charming friend of yours.'

This was a pleasant task and, Carina was sure, helped dispel some of the bad atmosphere after Marcus' visit.

When they had finished, they went along to the conservatory and found Taryn nodding in his chair.

He brightened at once on seeing Carina.

'Marcus didn't get his own way,' he said grimly. 'And he won't be on our guest list.'

Carina smiled, glad to see that the twinkle was still there in Taryn's old eyes as he smiled at his bride to be.

The message on the answer phone at Spray Point was brief and to the point. Carina stared at the machine in bewilderment, as if it could explain to her what it was all about.

'We're selling up,' Belinda's deep voice had announced. 'Phone me when you get in. We're here all afternoon.'

Carina replayed the message, unable to take in the implications. Had the events at the cliffs turned her brain, so that she was hearing imaginary voices? But, heard a third time, the message was no different. This was Belinda at her most succinct and what she was saying was incredible.

Belinda was mad. Or was she? The world was mad. A 98-year-old man getting married was mad. Marcus Trent issuing ultimatums and threatening letters from his solicitor was mad.

At this moment, what Carina wanted most in the world was to be back in her familiar Bristol life, in the warmth and comfort of her family and the place that had been home to her for as long as she could remember.

She took a deep breath as she walked across to the window. Outside, sunlight sparkled on the waves surging into the shore and the sand looked golden. There were people sunning themselves on the beach now that the fog had cleared. The surfers were out in force, too, weaving this way and that as they rode the waves. She wished she were relaxing in the sunshine instead of indoors at Spray Point trying to work out why Belinda had come to such a momentous decision. Maybe her husband was worse, had died, even. Oh no, not that! But Belinda had used the word we in her message and that could surely mean he was home again and they had made this decision together.

But standing here at the window was wasting time and there was nothing for it but to make the phone call. With a last glance at the brightness outside, Carina hastened to pick up the phone again and dial Belinda's home number.

The ringing tone continued for so long, she nearly gave up. But just as she was about to replace the receiver, Belinda's voice boomed out, 'Can I help you?'

'I don't know,' Carina said. 'I'm returning your call.'

She listened in growing dismay as Belinda told her that, after due consideration during the weeks her husband had been in hospital, they had made the joint decision to retire from the holiday letting business. This seemed a good moment to go ahead and put the properties on the market. In fact, their competitor, who owned one of the apartments in the same block on the other side of the beach, had already made a good offer on them and on the cottages as well, which they had accepted. There was no reason why things shouldn't move quickly.

'Spray Point?' asked Carina in a hoarse voice.

She heard the hesitation on the other end of the phone. 'Well, yes, Spray Point,' Belinda said. 'We're still discussing that.'

'So you won't need me to work for you when the sale goes through?'

'Obviously not.' Belinda sounded so matter of fact that a spurt of anger shot through Carina. What was it about her that encouraged people to go ahead with plans that would affect her without the decency to give her any inkling of what was in store?

'I see,' she said.

* * *

Afterwards, she thought she should have asked at what point her contract would be terminated, but she had felt too numb to think of it.

She would do no more work today after hearing this, she thought. The unexpectedness of it had knocked her for six and she felt fit for nothing. She was owed a few hours to herself, anyway. Belinda would just have to put up with it.

Carina left Spray Point, making for the headland instead of going the other way into town, not wanting to see anyone she knew until she had thought this thing through. She couldn't bear to hear Annabel ranting against Belinda at this moment, dear as her friend was to her.

She just wanted to be by herself to try to come to terms with what was happening.

She trudged on, head down, seeing nothing of her surroundings and was surprised when she reached the end of the headland. She raised her face to the cleansing air blowing in from the Atlantic.

Temporary work should be easy to find now that the season was under way, she reasoned. She owed Belinda nothing.

She had done good work for her and now she felt betrayed, worthless. She would pack up and leave, knowing her absence would no longer have the same impact on her great-uncle because he had his beloved Rosa, soon to become his wife. She could visit every now and again, after all.

She had seen how valuable Rob was to Jamie, so dependable and able to take charge of difficult situations when needed. She shuddered as she thought of him in the thickness of the fog and the darkness of the cave as he worked to free Zena's foot and help her out in safety, knowing that at any moment the tide could come sweeping in. Rob was brave and strong and . . . a sob tore at her throat.

At last she allowed herself to admit what she felt, perhaps had always felt.

She loved Rob. Had always loved him, but had fought against it because he so obviously didn't love her. Sometimes, she thought, he didn't even seem to like her much.

So she would go away.

Her decision would please Marcus Trent and his mother who were her blood relations, but who didn't care for her any more than she cared for them.

She turned her back to the wind and walked slowly back the way she had come, seeing now quite clearly that the people who meant the most to her were not the people she had found down here.

The only exception was her great-uncle, Taryn Curnow. By coming to Cornwall, she had found him.

Her sense of worthlessness began to fade as she dwelt on that.

THE FUTURE LOOKS BRIGHT

Carina stopped, startled, as she saw a car parked at the bottom of the steps at Spray Point. What was Sadie's blue Honda Jazz doing here when she should be in the Exe estuary, her binoculars clamped to her eyes? Then she remembered. Rob had the use of the car while his mother was unable to drive. She could see him now, seated on the stone wall that bordered the grassy terrace at the bottom of the steps. He looked as if he had been there some time.

She steeled herself to approach him.

'Rob,' she said lightly, 'What are you doing here?'

He leapt up when he saw her. 'I came to find you, Carina.' His shorts and T-shirt accentuated his tanned limbs and his eyes looked very blue.

She gazed at him, breathless for no apparent reason. He seemed in no hurry to say anything more, but looked around, as if sizing up the property.

'You haven't come to make an offer on Spray Point, have you?' she said, a tartness in her voice because of the surprise of seeing him.

He swung round, amused. 'I can certainly see that the place has potential. A bit of a dump at the moment, I grant you, but with money spent on it, it could be made into a fine home.'

'Not for my employer,' Carina said, trying not to sound bitter. 'Belinda's decided to sell the business. I expect Spray Point will go, too, and I can't bear to think about it.'

'You like it here?'

She nodded. 'I love it.'

'Then I wish I could buy it for you.' His tone was light.

'Please don't joke about it, Rob,' she said with a catch in her voice. 'Belinda's already had an offer on all the holiday properties.'

'So Belinda really is selling up? Good.'

'Good?' Carina looked at him in surprise.

She had enjoyed her job here in spite of the hard work and had gained immense satisfaction from pleasing the clients. She was coming to see that this place could provide all she wanted, not just for a few weeks but for the foreseeable future. All that now was to be taken from her.

And Rob said it was good.

'You've lost me,' she said. 'It all seems bad to me.'

'I've been hearing rumours flying about for a day or two,' he said. 'And now I've had time to think things through.'

'So I was the last to know about Belinda's plans. How fair is that?' She pulled a paper tissue from her pocket, screwed it into a small

193

ball and then stuffed it back again.

'I think you should find out from your employers exactly where you stand in all this. It might well be that the purchaser will agree to keep you on. You know where Belinda lives?'

She nodded. 'Loveday Close.'

'I know it.' He indicated the car. 'Shall we go?'

She did as he invited, reminded of the time he had picked her up from her evening class. Then, he had been driving her home. Now, she didn't know what was going to happen, and it was good to let Rob take charge. She glanced at him as they drove off, seeing the determination on his face.

Belinda's house was set back from the road in a quiet cul de sac. Rob parked the car in the drive. 'Come on.'

He walked resolutely to the front door, which was immediately opened. Carina, following behind, thought that Belinda looked less strained today. Not surprising, if the worry about her husband's health had lifted.

He was in the sitting room at the back of the house, resting in a reclining chair that seemed too short for his long legs. The deep sofas looked far more comfortable but his chair was nearer the television set and also close to an overflowing bookcase that looked as if it had plenty of use. A pair of spectacles and The Times newspaper lay on a low table nearby.

'Don't get up,' said Rob.

'This is Carina, who's living at Spray Point,' Belinda said. 'Carina, my husband, Mark.' She turned to Rob. 'And you are?'

'A friend with Carina's interests at heart.'

'I guessed as much,' Mark Penberthy said. 'Sit down, both of you. I've been hearing how well this young lady has been coping while I've been in hospital. She's helped my wife in more ways than she'll ever know.'

Belinda pulled forward a chair and plumped down on it. 'He's right, you know.'

Her husband smiled at Carina. 'I'm sorry it's come to this, my dear, but we had no alternative. And I think Belinda has something to offer you to show her appreciation.'

Carina was speechless. This was totally unexpected.

'It's Mark's idea,' Belinda said, a smile on her lips as she looked at her husband. 'It's Spray Point.'

'Spray Point?' Carina looked from one to the other in bewilderment. 'I don't understand.'

'Spray Point was going to be our dream home,' Mark Penberthy said. 'I'd been doing well in the City and Belinda wanted to come back to Cornwall to live. But we soon saw it wouldn't do, and when this place came on the market, we moved in. We used Spray Point as a store when we set up our holiday letting business and let the place go rather.

'We have no children,' Mark Penberthy went on with sadness. 'And Belinda agrees with me. We're comfortably off and we don't need the money. We've been able to sell the business as a going concern because of you, my dear, for a much higher price than we expected. We're well pleased. And this is our way of saying thank you.'

'You don't mean . . .' Carina broke off, unable to voice what she was beginning to suspect. Beginning to hope.

'We'd like to give Spray Point to you, my dear.'

'But . . . but you can't give it away just like that,' Carina objected.

'A lot needs doing to it, we know. It's been neglected for years.'

'Oh no, I couldn't . . .'

'So you don't think it's a good idea?' Mark said.

'Oh yes, of course I do. But I can't accept it.'

'You have no choice in the matter,' Belinda's husband said. 'We've already decided. You can put it on the market yourself, my dear, if you so choose. We've begun to put the change of ownership in motion. There will be papers to sign in due course. We'd like you to have it, young lady.'

Carina got unsteadily to her feet. 'I can't quite take all this in yet but . . . thank you, I'll come again another day to say thank you properly.'

Mark looked pleased and on impulse Carina leaned forward and kissed his cheek.

*　　*　　*

Carina and Rob walked in silence back to the car.

'I can't believe this,' Carina whispered.

'I would have given Spray Point to you,' Rob said.

She was so bemused she hardly heard him.

They drove back to Spray Point. Carina got out of the car and stared up at the white building above them. The front of the place was in shadow but there was a glimmer about it, as if it knew how things had changed. The evening air was soft now the wind had dropped, but behind her the sea still roared.

'I could always sell it,' she said.

'You'd do that?'

'If I'd known about this sooner, I could have invested the money in something.'

The silence felt heavy between them. She knew without looking at him that Rob was gazing at Spray Point, too.

'Do you mean *Leapaway*?' he said.

'It means so much to Jamie.'

'And to others who'll be working for him.'

'I was devastated at the threat Marcus made,' she said. 'I had to choose what to do.'

'Jamie told me all this,' Rob said quietly. 'I know you care about him. I understood your anguish at putting your great-uncle first, so I decided I must do something about it myself. I couldn't bear your pain, Carina, but I had to act fast in order to organise my finances and contact my friends in New Zealand to tell them I'd decided to stay.

'It was easier done from Bristol, so I left.'

'So you're the investor who saved *Leapaway*?' Carina said, hardly able to believe it.

'I wanted to help. I was attracted to the concept of *Leapaway* from the beginning, as you know. And I also know that your business expertise will be invaluable.' He shrugged. 'It's just money.'

'But it's your money.'

'Look, I'd appreciate it if we keep this a secret between the three of us. I'll keep out of your way as much as possible, Carina. I wish you and Jamie well.'

He turned to go, and in that moment, Carina knew what she had to do.

'It's not Jamie,' she blurted out. 'It's not Jamie who's important to me.'

Rob took a step towards her. 'It's not?'

'There's nothing between us now. I came to realise . . . and he did too. No, it's not Jamie.'

He hesitated.

'Rob,' she murmured. 'Oh Rob.'

The next moment she was in his arms. He bent and kissed her for a beautiful, long moment.

198

She pulled away, trembling.

'What's wrong?' he said softly.

'I'm living a dream,' she told him happily.

He laughed and the sound was wonderful. How had it taken her so long to realise Rob was the one she loved all this time?

'Let's continue the dream,' he said. 'Let's walk for a while and talk about us. I'm not going to let you go now, Carrie, my love. We've plans to make. Look, the sea's beautiful with the streaks of pink in it on the horizon and the wind's dropped. We'll go to the end of the headland.'

The calm sea reflected the evening colours of the setting sun. The turf felt soft beneath Carina's feet and the scent of thyme filled the air. This would be with her forever, she thought. Through all the bad times and the good, she would remember this perfect moment.

'I have a suggestion to make,' Rob said, as he smiled down at her. 'A good one, if I may say so.'

'Ever the arrogant one.'

'How about this then . . . a double wedding with your great-uncle and Rosa at that little stone church at Madrenna in a few week's time? The reception at Madrenna Nursing Home, d'you think? The perfect venue.

'And Carina, my perfect love, will you marry me?'

'I don't see how I could refuse.'

He laughed and kissed her again.

'So what do you think?'

'Perfect,' she said.

*   *   *

She'd take Rob with her to visit her great-uncle and Rosa and have wonderful news to tell them. They would be as overjoyed for her as she was for them.

Rob smiled. 'You'll have your other relations as well, my love, Mercenary Marcus and his doting mother.'

Carina shuddered. 'No way.'

Rob grinned. 'But Mum and Annabel and Dave will come to the wedding,' he said. 'And all the *Leapaway* crowd we'll be working with.'

'All the people we feel really close to,' she agreed.

Suddenly, in the distance, a shower of light, red and blue and gold, shot into the dusky sky.

'There they are,' Rob said, 'celebrating with us already.'

As if in answer, another burst of colour filled the sky above the beach. They watched, entranced, until the fireworks were finished.

'But what will Sadie think about having the wedding here?' Carina said.

'Mum will be delighted. I think we'd better

drive up tomorrow to this place, Woodbury, and see what she says, don't you? I've a feeling she'll want us to do a bit of house-hunting down here for her before long. A useful base for us while we oversee the alterations at Spray Point to make it our home.'

Carina laughed. 'Perfect. But I hope Sadie thinks so, too. She'll be losing a son.'

'But gaining a daughter.'

'I've always been that,' she pointed out, 'A pretend one, anyway.'

'Then things will be just the same.'

'Not for me,' Carina said. 'For me, things are so wonderfully different.'

Even the very air was different, so clear and sweet-scented. And as Rob folded her in his arms Carina knew she could look forward to a lifetime of happiness.